Satisfied, she str

water. Her wet chemise clung to her frame, and she knew Lord Seacrest was getting a lordly eyeful right now. Her nipples were rock-hard from the cold.

She rolled her eyes toward the bright, blue sky. *My kingdom for a bra! And throw in a pair of underwear, too!* But both articles of clothing were back at Nihtscua and not likely to appear anytime soon. For the first time since plunging into the surf, she regarded Hugh.

Eyes wide, her dry smock clutched in his hands, he stood as if frozen. Only his gaze moved, traveling from her breasts to the apex of her thighs.

She pulled the smock away from her flesh as best she could and advanced toward him, stopping an arm's length away. "I told you I could swim."

He blinked. Then his full, sensual lips curled into a smile. "Indeed, you did."

"And?"

"And what?"

"You've doubted me twice already. Perhaps you owe me an apology."

His eyes widened, then relaxed. "Perhaps I do. Pray…forgive me."

The words couldn't have come easily, and the fact he'd said them made her grin. "I forgive you. This time. But I ask respectfully that you not underestimate me again."

For two seconds, he hesitated. "'Tis a reasonable request, and I shall endeavor to honor it." He gave her a quizzical look. Then he shook his head and chuckled. "Is there anything you cannot do?"

Praise for Judith Sterling

"Judith Sterling creates a beautiful, poetic mood that flows through the whole story... The author describes every environment perfectly and vividly brings every emotion to life... *Flight of the Raven* (The Novels of Ravenwood, Book One) is a fantastic book for lovers of historical romance and romance alike!"

~*~

~InD'Tale Magazine

"*Soul of the Wolf* (The Novels of Ravenwood, Book Two) is a sweeping historical romance that transported me to Medieval England!!"

~N. N. Light's Book Heaven

~*~

"*Shadow of the Swan* (The Novels of Ravenwood, Book Three) will transform you and reaffirm the power of love."

~N. N. Light's Book Heaven;
Best Historical Romance of 2018 nomination

~*~

"Drop what you're doing and read *The Cauldron Stirred* (Guardians of Erin, Book One) now!"

~N. N. Light's Book Heaven;
Best Paranormal of 2018 Award

~*~

"Readers of *The Stone Awakened* (Guardians of Erin, Book Two) will be caught up in Judith Sterling's magical world filled with modern, relatable characters, Irish legends, mystical creatures, sweet romance, and a suspenseful mystery leaving them with hungry anticipation for the next book in the series."

~InD'Tale Magazine, 2019 RONE Award nomination

Night of the Owl

by

Judith Sterling

The Novels of Ravenwood, Book 4

Night of the Owl

Cover Art by *Debbie Taylor*

The Wild Rose Press, Inc.
PO Box 708
Adams Basin, NY 14410-0708
Visit us at www.thewildrosepress.com

Publishing History
First Tea Rose Edition, 2019
Print ISBN 978-1-5092-2815-7
Digital ISBN 978-1-5092-2816-4

The Novels of Ravenwood, Book 4
Published in the United States of America

Dedication

I dedicate this book to my beautiful, intelligent,
talented, determined, and open-hearted niece,
Becca.
From one Sterling to another, I am so proud of
all your accomplishments
and the lovely young woman you've become.
This one's for you!

Chapter One

Northumberland, England
July 1986

For the love of God, stay awake! It's not much farther. Ardyth Nightshade gripped the steering wheel of her rental car and yawned, bringing welcome tears to her dry, scratchy eyes as she continued driving north.

The morning traffic was unremarkable. Nonexistent compared to rush hour in Chicago. Even so, driving on the left side of narrow roads flanked by stone walls waiting to crush one at the slightest mistake required all the focus she could muster. If only she'd been able to sleep on the plane!

Excitement forbade it, on both the overseas flight to London and the connecting one to Newcastle. Ruled by adrenaline, she'd daydreamed the hours away. A PhD student in medieval studies couldn't ask for a better summer job than the one she'd landed. Not only would she work as research assistant to Professor Henri Seacrest, but after two long decades, she was finally returning to her father's ancestral home. Memories from childhood—some vague, others clear and resonant—had made Nightshade Manor synonymous with magic. She itched to see the place again.

Now she was paying for her eagerness, craving caffeine, and sporting dark circles under her eyes. She cast a second glance at the rearview mirror, in the hope that her first was too critical.

It wasn't. Long but limp blonde hair. Shadows beneath her brown eyes. Next to no redeeming makeup. She'd worn only foundation, just enough to keep from scaring small children on the flight, and then the airline lost her makeup case. Better that than her clothes, but still...

At least she wore a new skirt and blouse. Travel had wrinkled them a bit, but there was no possibility of ironing them now. No way to cover the fresh scuff on her right shoe either.

With a sigh of acceptance, she returned her attention to the road. *I'll make one hell of an impression on my new boss. If I can keep my eyes open long enough to get there.* She cranked up the radio and sang along with Madonna's "Papa Don't Preach."

Like a beacon of mercy, the ruins of Nihtscua Castle—her ancestors' earlier home—came into view. High on a throne of rock, the ancient keep held vigil over the modern town of Prestby, the merger of the medieval villages of Preostbi and Nihtscua. Most of the buildings dated to the eighteenth and nineteenth centuries. Relatively new to a history buff like her...and her professors...and PhD candidates like...

No! She refused to blight her summer with thoughts of her ex-boyfriend. This was her time, her adventure. Afterward, she would return to the university in glory, and no one would interfere with her academic career. Not even that rank-stank piece of...

Let it go!

The castle towered above as she braked before its entrance path. She couldn't wait to explore the place again. *Later,* she promised herself. *First things first.*

She turned right and drove the short distance up the hill to the manor. The gates were open, so she went on through, followed the circular driveway toward the house, and parked right in front. Her pulse quickened as she stepped out of the car and gazed upward.

Nightshade Manor was everything an Elizabethan home should be: built of stone and crowned by a multitude of chimneys reaching toward the soft morning sky. Its large, mullioned windows beckoned, and she hastened to the great oak door. She lifted her hand to knock, but the door swung open before she made contact.

A marvel of masculinity stood before her. It was as if the doorway existed for the sole purpose of framing his tall, broad-shouldered frame. His short, black hair framed a clean-shaven face whose smooth, hard lines set the stage for a full, sensuous mouth and wide, gray eyes. Despite his casual attire of jeans and a blue, button-down shirt, he oozed authority…and more sex appeal than she'd ever encountered up close.

After a heart-stopping moment, she found her voice. "Professor Seacrest?"

He enfolded her upraised hand with both of his. Their warmth flowed into her as his steady gaze held hers.

"Please, call me Henri." A French accent laced his words. "You must be Ardyth."

I must? Argh! Don't be an idiot. "Yes."

She hadn't expected him to be so young. Mid-thirties at most. Her father had made him sound quite distinguished, which he must be to convince her parents to let him spend the entire summer in their home while

3

researching Anglo-Saxon sites. Of course, her mom and dad were currently back in Illinois, in the house where she'd lived most of her life.

Henri still held her hand. She looked down at it and cleared her throat.

Quickly, he released it. "Forgive me."

"No problem. Anyway, thank you for this opportunity."

His pupils dilated, inviting her into their inky depths. "It is I who am thankful to work with *you*. Your record at the University of Chicago is impressive, as is your knowledge of Anglo-Saxon and Anglo-Norman. Few are fluent in both."

"Well, when your dad's a medieval history professor and your mom loves dead languages…"

"Yes, you were raised in a trilingual home. But most parents speak living languages with their children."

She shrugged. "I didn't know any different. And it was kind of fun switching back and forth between the medieval languages and Modern English. I never realized we were unique until I started elementary school—or primary school, as they call it here—and my classmates filled me in."

"Well, I can read Anglo-Norman, but your facility for Anglo-Saxon will be a great help."

"And I suppose it doesn't hurt that this is my family's house. I mean, Dad's American, but he inherited this from his grandfather."

He nodded, then glanced toward the rental car. "Do you have luggage?"

"Two suitcases in the trunk, but I can get them." She turned, strode to the car, and opened the trunk…or "boot" as the Brits called it.

In a flash, he was at her side. "Allow me."

"It's really not necessary."

"I insist." Reaching past her, he grabbed the bags, then started toward the house.

Okay, if it means that much to you. Knock yourself out. With a yawn, she closed the lid and followed him to the door.

He paused in front of it. "After you."

The guy was a gentleman; she had to give him that. Actually, she might be tempted to give him a lot more, if she wasn't careful. But no. She was done with men, at least for the foreseeable future. Her career was top priority. She'd make a name for herself, just as her father had, before he retired to write fiction. Maybe if he'd hung around the department a little longer, John wouldn't have gotten away with…

"Miss Nightshade?"

"Oh. Sorry."

She stepped inside and scanned the entrance hall. It was just as she remembered. The flagstone floor. Oak paneling. Exposed beams. The majestic staircase with shallow steps and richly carved newel post and balustrade.

Thud! The door had closed. She turned to see Henri watching her.

"Is it all that you remembered?" His voice held a note of longing.

She blinked. "Pretty much. I was six the last time I was here."

"Yes, your father told me." He started up the stairs, and she kept pace with him. "You may have your old room, if you like. Or your parents' bedroom. Hannah made both ready."

"Ah, sweet Hannah. It'll be good to see her again. I guess she and Frank still live in town?" The couple had been caretakers of Nightshade Manor for as long as she could remember.

"They do."

Ardyth's stomach quivered. *Then it's just you and I here. Alone.* "I'll use my parents' room, since it's bigger." *Thank God it has a private bath!*

"Very well."

They reached the top of the stairs and continued down the hall. Portraits of her ancestors observed their progress.

At last, Henri entered her parents' bedroom and set her luggage at the foot of the four-poster bed that was even older than the house. The story was, it once graced Nihtscua Castle's main bedchamber. He glanced toward the stone fireplace, then met her gaze. "Would you care to take a walk? Perhaps up to the site of the runestone?"

Was that a catch in his voice? As though he'd tried a little too hard to sound casual?

Ridiculous. I'm imagining things. A lion's yawn overtook her, and she shook her head. "Maybe later. Right now, if you don't mind, I need a nap."

A slight frown crossed his features, but he quickly replaced it with a congenial smile. "Of course. You have had a long journey. It is...good to have you here...Ardyth."

His eyes smoldered. Heat suffused her cheeks and forehead.

"Thanks. It's good to be here."

He crossed to the door, hesitated on the threshold, and turned back to her. "Sleep well." Then he left, closing the door behind him.

With a sigh, she glanced around the room. It felt strangely empty without the professor's commanding presence. Or maybe she just missed her parents. She'd call them later to let them know she arrived safely.

Sleep was the immediate goal. She kicked off her shoes, removed her blouse, skirt, bra, slip, and pantyhose, and dug through one of her suitcases for her Chicago Cubs nightshirt. Slipping into it, she yawned again, then threw back the bedcovers and slid between the cool, cotton sheets. Minutes later, she rested in the arms of Morpheus.

Knock! Knock! Knock!

Ardyth woke with a start, then remembered where she was. A feeling of rightness settled over her. With a contented sigh, she rolled over and glimpsed the clock on the nightstand. It was noon. She'd slept only two hours.

Knock! Knock! Knock!

So that's what woke me. Was it Hannah? Her husband, Frank? Or…

She threw back the covers and shuffled to the door. Realizing her toothbrush and toothpaste were in her missing makeup case, she rolled her eyes. *Nothing like dragon breath to give you confidence.* She opened the door.

Henri flashed a smile. Then his gaze dropped to the nightshirt that revealed most of her legs. "I…" His gaze shot back to hers. "I wondered if you were awake."

"I am now."

"Shall we walk then?"

Aren't you an eager beaver? "Somehow I thought you'd want me to dive right into the old documents.

Dad told me you're also interested in the connection between the Nightshade and Ravenwood lines."

He nodded. "I want to trace the Ravenwood link to the Seacrests of North Yorkshire."

"Right. Dad said you were related to them."

He looked past her into the bedroom. "Distantly. So…about that walk…"

"Sure, but first, I'm in desperate need of a shower. By the way, the airline lost some of my stuff, so I'll have to shop for a few essentials later. In the meantime, can I borrow your toothpaste?" Without a toothbrush, her finger would have to suffice.

"Of course. One moment." He hurried down the hall to a guest bedroom. Returning a minute later, he handed her the tube of toothpaste. "Here."

"Thanks. I'll be ready in a jiffy."

After a quick shower, she cleaned her teeth as best she could, blew-dry her hair, and donned jeans, a pink top, and tennis shoes. Then she rushed into the hall and stopped short.

At the head of the stairs stood Henri, staring at her. "You are ready?"

With a casual stride, she approached him. "Yeah, but I have to ask…have you been standing there waiting this whole time?"

He averted his gaze. "No. Of course not." Turning, he started down the stairs, and she shadowed him. "But I am anxious to show you an interesting carving I found on the ancient steps near the runestone."

"Which steps? The ones to the underground chamber?"

"No. The others."

"Oh. The stairway to nowhere. It used to fascinate

me. When I was six, I tried to climb it, but my mom freaked out and wouldn't let me. She never explained why. We moved to the States soon after that."

They reached the base of the stairs and continued toward the back of the quiet house.

She smiled. "It's funny, but I always wished I'd climbed those stairs."

"Now you have the chance to fulfill that wish."

"Yeah. It's been a long time coming."

They walked on in silence until he opened the back door. "After you."

"Thanks." She stepped outside.

The sun and scents of the knot garden welcomed her home. With its gravel paths, clipped box hedges, and colorful flowerbeds, it was a masterwork of beauty and order. The sweet smell of roses filled her senses, even as the click-clack of shifting pebbles beneath her feet conjured memories. When she'd played hide-and-seek with her father in the garden, that same sound foretold his imminent discovery of her hiding places. Hugs and laughter always followed.

She made a sweeping gesture with her hands. "Frank has really kept things up."

Henri closed the back door and joined her on the path. "So he has."

They strode to the far side of the garden and ascended the steps that led up the side of the hill to a stretch of woods. Elms, beeches, birches, and oaks shivered all around as a cool breeze tempted their leaves into motion.

She grinned. "I used to think this was an enchanted forest."

"I understand why." He returned her smile.

Her stomach dropped, and she tripped on a protruding root. "Oh!"

He caught her arm. "Are you all right?"

He was too handsome for his own good. Or rather, for hers. "Yeah. I'm fine."

His hand lingered a moment, then dropped from her arm. "Watch your step. We are nearly there."

A minute later, they came to the clearing, around which soaring evergreens formed a circle. Inside it to the left, the runestone topped a grassy knoll whose gaping entrance led to the underground chamber. To the right was the mysterious staircase, seven feet wide and twenty steps high.

She stopped and stared. Weathered yet enduring, the stone steps riveted her, called to her on a level she couldn't ignore. "You said there's a carving you wanted to show me?"

"Up on the landing."

"Is it a symbol?"

He pointed. "Go to the top, and you will see."

For a moment, she felt six years old again. But there was no one to stop her this time. With a grin, she bounded up the steps.

She paused on the landing and studied its scoured, gray surface. Frowning, she turned to look down at the professor. "I don't see anything."

His gaze was intense. Unaccountably so. "It is there, at the very edge. Go a bit farther."

"Okay." She took three more steps, then halted as her feet began to tingle. "What the hell?" The sensation traveled up her legs. Heat claimed her entire body, and she felt rooted to the stone. A powerful vibration took hold.

****

She vanished before his eyes. His chest tightened. Then a long sigh escaped his lips. Turning, he started back toward the house.

A storm of emotions raged inside him. Had it worked? Was she safe? What if…

No! He refused to entertain doubts. All would be well. It must be.

Hope held his focus. So much so, he barely noticed the trees, the garden, or any part of the manor that wasn't the telephone in the study. He lifted the receiver and dialed the number he knew by heart.

"It is done," he said after a moment. "Now we wait."

Chapter Two

The vibration ceased. Ardyth blinked, then turned to the professor.

He was gone.

"Henri!" She looked around, but he was nowhere. Not in the clearing, nor among the thick wall of trees. "What the…"

A glittering sight below grabbed her attention. Beneath the runestone, in the side of the mound, was a lavishly decorated door of gold.

She gaped at it as she descended the stairs. "Where did *you* come from?"

"Good day to you."

She whirled to her left, where a young girl—perhaps ten years old—stood at the rim of the forest. Blonde and blue-eyed, she hugged a bundle of cloth to her torso, which was clad in a long tunic of cornflower blue. Such garments were worn in the High Middle Ages.

Ardyth frowned. *Is there some renaissance festival in the area? If so, what's she doing here, on our property?*

Then it hit her. *She spoke Anglo-Saxon!*

The girl's gaze traveled the length of Ardyth's body, down to the tennis shoes and back up to the jeans. "Whence have you come?" She tilted her head. "Or mayhap I should ask, from *when*?" She spoke in a lower voice, as if to herself.

When? Is she talking about time travel? Ardyth shook her head. *I'm dreaming.* She pinched her arm, then squeezed her eyes shut and opened them again.

The girl was still there. "Perhaps you'll understand this better. Welcome to Nihtscua. My name is Freya. What is yours?"

And that was Anglo-Norman! "M-my name is Ardyth," she replied in the same language.

Never was she more grateful to her parents for her unusual linguistic skills than in this moment. Had they known this would happen? Or guessed it might? Is that why her mother had whisked her away from the stairs when she tried to climb them all those years ago?

More like, all those years in the future. Her mind reeled.

Freya beamed at her. "I knew you were coming. That is, I knew *someone* was. Someone of my blood."

"Coming whither exactly? That is, to when?"

"The month of July, in the year of our Lord eleven hundred and two."

You've got to be kidding me! She slipped again into Anglo-Norman. "Do you jest?"

"Not at all."

Her legs felt shaky, tense, but she shook them out. "How did you know I was coming?"

"I have the Sight…or something like it. Rather than seeing things, I simply know them. All at once, without even trying."

"You said I was someone of your blood. Do you live in the castle?"

Freya nodded. "I'm Wulfstan's…that is, Lord Nihtscua's sister, and these…" She handed Ardyth the bundle she'd been holding. "…are Jocelyn's…Lady Nihtscua's garments. I dare not take you to the keep in the strange clothing you now wear. 'Tis vital that you blend in."

"I'm sure you're right." Ardyth examined the medieval clothes. Low leather boots, linen hose and smock, and both an inner tunic and outer one in shades of green.

"You may dress here." Freya turned her back. "I shan't look, and there's no one else around."

Quickly, Ardyth changed. She had to admit the tunics were more comfortable than her jeans, but the stockings and boots couldn't compete with her modern socks and tennis shoes. Without underwear, she felt a bit exposed yet free.

"Done," she announced. "What should I do with my old clothing?"

Turning, Freya grabbed the clothes in question and marched toward the mound. She opened the golden door, then disappeared down the stairs. Half a minute later, she reappeared and shut the door behind her. "I've hidden them in the Wolf Stone chamber."

"The Wolf Stone." Ardyth pointed to the runestone. "Is that what you call it?"

"Aye." With a smile, Freya gestured to the high, stone staircase, which looked considerably newer than its twentieth-century counterpart. "And that is Woden's Stair. Come. You must meet my brother."

Ardyth followed her onto the same woodland path she'd trodden with the professor mere minutes before, but the medieval forest was far more expansive. It extended even beyond the plot of the Elizabethan Manor, which wouldn't exist for another five hundred years.

At last, the forest fell away, revealing a bustling village everyone in her medieval studies program would kill to see. *But I'm the one who's here. If this is really happening!* Tall, sunlit peaks and heather-covered moorland—some of which would one day become World War II-era housing—rose in the distance.

"This way." Freya turned right and started up the hill toward the gatehouse.

Ardyth's jaw dropped when she glimpsed the castle. No longer a ruin, its battlements and four corner towers were perfectly intact, and a wooden curtain wall surrounded the whole.

A trio of peasant women walking down the hill cast curious glances her way. Was it because her hair flowed freely down her back? Or because she was a stranger in fine clothing?

"Almost there," Freya encouraged her.

They crossed the drawbridge and entered the gatehouse. A large, bald gatekeeper flashed Freya a smile that lacked several teeth.

"I'm back, Offa, and I've brought a guest."

Offa's gaze moved to Ardyth and remained there.

She gave him a closed-mouth grin. "Good day to you, Offa."

The gatekeeper's eyes widened. "Er…good day."

Freya tugged on her hand. "Make haste."

The noise of the crowded bailey slammed into Ardyth as they exited the gatehouse. She'd imagined such activity when exploring the ruins as a little girl—and later, during research at college—but the reality stole her breath. Whether laundering clothes, tending the garden, chasing chickens, or fetching water from the well, every servant was bent to his or her task. Anglo-Saxon chatter and shouts, the neighing of horses, the grunt of pigs, together with the smells of hay and roasting meat, added to the mix.

In a daze, she continued. *This is no dream. It's real!*

Freya led her through the swarm and up the broad, stone steps to the keep's entrance. The oaken double doors were impressive, but the great hall was even more so, with tapestries and banners galore. A handful of servants scrubbed the floor, while others spread a fine, white cloth on the table atop the dais.

"Wow," Ardyth breathed in Modern English.

Freya turned to her. "What did you say?"

Right. The Great Vowel Shift is still centuries away. They have their own version of "wow," but that specific word doesn't exist yet. "Nothing," she said in Anglo-Norman. "Is your brother here?"

Freya scanned the hall, then pointed. "There! With his wife." She hastened toward a striking couple at the far side of the hall.

Like his sister, the man was blond and dressed in blue. He was also incredibly handsome. The lovely redhead who clasped his hand wore a yellow gown that might've been an extension of her fiery hair.

Man, I come from good genes! Then her stomach lurched. *But will they welcome me or throw me in the dungeon? What on earth do I say to them?* Maybe it was best to simply follow their lead. She took a deep breath and hurried to catch up with Freya.

"Wulfstan! Jocelyn!" Freya stopped in front of them, then turned back to Ardyth. "May I present

Ardyth? Ardyth, this is Lord and Lady Nihtscua."

Two pairs of eyes—the lady's brown, the lord's an arresting ice blue—looked her up and down. Heat flooded her cheeks as Wulfstan's unwavering gaze held hers.

Say something! "I'm pleased to meet you."

"Are those my garments?" Jocelyn asked.

Freya nodded. "Aye, but we had no choice."

Wulfstan raised an eyebrow, then regarded his sister. "We? I confess, I feel an odd sense of connection with her, but...who is she?"

With a grin, Freya placed a hand on Jocelyn's belly. "The result of this."

Jocelyn's brow furrowed. "What do you mean?"

Freya lowered her voice to a conspiratorial whisper. "She's your descendant. She came by way of Woden's Stair. I hid her own clothing in the Wolf Stone chamber."

Jocelyn's hands flew to her stomach, and her eyes widened. "Wondrous! You knew she'd be there, didn't you?"

Freya grinned. "I did."

Wulfstan nodded slowly. "Now I understand. You're very welcome...Ardyth, was it?"

"Aye. Ardyth Nightshade. That's my family name, derived from Nihtscua."

"Fascinating." He glanced around the hall, then started forward. "Come, all of you. Let's talk in the solar." He led her back across the hall, with Jocelyn and Freya close behind, and through an archway near the dais.

Ardyth smiled, drinking in the solar's warmth. It looked so "lived in," which made perfect sense, of course. This wasn't a windswept shell of bygone days; these were those days! Tapestries and cushioned seats added color to the room. Sunlight poured through the open shutters. Candles, cards, game boards, and half-finished needlework waited on the tables for day's end.

He motioned to two high-backed chairs before the dormant hearth. "Pray, sit." He put a hand on Jocelyn's back. "You too, my dear." Once the women were seated, he moved two stools to rest in front of them. Then he motioned to Freya, and they sat as well.

On the edge of her chair, Jocelyn leaned forward. "I must ask…from what year have you come?"

Amazing! Her eyes are the exact shade of mine and Dad's. "Nineteen hundred and eighty-six."

Those eyes nearly doubled in size. "But…that's more than eight hundred years hence!"

Wulfstan whistled. "Incredible. Does Nihtscua stand in your time?"

She nodded. "It does, as a ruin. There's a newer house on the property, which was built…that is, it *will* be built in sixteen hundred and two."

"And the land still belongs to our family?"

"As improbable as it seems, aye."

"I'm glad to hear it. But I wonder…why did Woden's Stair bring you so far back? What purpose does your presence here serve?"

Freya sat up straight. "Meg will know."

He turned to her. "Meg?"

"I'm certain of it." She looked to Ardyth. "The woman of whom I speak has prophetic dreams, and I've no doubt she's foreseen your coming." She turned back to her brother. "You must send word to her immediately. She'll know what to do."

He regarded Ardyth. "Meg, or Lady Margaret, is of the Ravenwood line. Normally, she lives at Ravenwood, but at present, she's staying at Druid's Head, not ten miles south of here. Have you heard of either estate?"

"I saw them in ruins when I was a little girl. My mother was a Ravenwood."

Jocelyn's brow furrowed. "Was? Is she…"

Ardyth shook her head. "No, she's very much alive. Ravenwood was her name before she married my father and took his name."

Freya tapped her foot on the ground. "Brother, listen to me. Write to Meg with all haste, and send your fastest rider to Druid's Head."

"Right." He stood. "Meanwhile, the two of you must show Ardyth around the keep." With powerful strides, he started off on his errand.

Freya jumped to her feet and called after him. "Your workroom too?"

He stopped short in the archway and turned back to them. "No, not there. But there's plenty to see elsewhere."

Jocelyn and Freya showed her everything but the tower room where, they explained, Wulfstan worked his magic. They didn't specify what kind, and Ardyth didn't press the point. She was too busy relishing the sights and sounds of the medieval world she'd only studied until now. Some of the smells—particularly those of human sweat and animal excrement—she could've done without, but they served to emphasize the fact that her experience was real. From basement to battlements, the keep was a marvel, and so were the people within it.

Just before supper, Meg's reply arrived, and Ardyth, Jocelyn, and Freya gathered around Wulfstan in the solar to hear it. He cleared his throat and read aloud:

" 'My dear Wulfstan, long have I awaited these tidings. 'Tis essential you heed my counsel. Sir Robert leaves on the morrow to visit his eldest brother Hugh, Lord Seacrest. Lady Constance is traveling with him, and so must Ardyth. Escort her to Druid's Head at daybreak and introduce her as Lady Ardyth, your kinswoman. I shall prepare Sir Robert for her coming and impress upon him and Lady Constance the importance of Ardyth's journey. I shall not, however, tell them whence she came. That will remain our secret, at least for the present. She shall return to her own time through the magic of Woden's Circle, but not before she visits Seacrest. She must stay there even after Sir Robert and Lady Constance return home. Hugh has been seeking a scribe to write his family's history, and Ardyth can serve in that capacity. I, myself, return to Ravenwood this very day, and I shall be there to see your descendant safely home. Ardyth will know instinctively the moment when she should return to her own time. Prithee, do as I ask. Much depends upon it. Yours ever, Meg.' "

Lord Nihtscua looked up from the parchment and into Ardyth's eyes. "Have you the skill to serve as a scribe?"

Ardyth thought for a moment. Thanks to summer courses in calligraphy and illuminated manuscript making, she just might pull it off. *Let's see...at this period, they haven't started using Gothic Black Letter yet. I could try Proto-Gothic, but it's probably safest to stick with English Caroline Miniscule Compressed.* "I believe so."

He rubbed his chin. "Impressive."

"I don't mean to doubt your judgment, but…you truly trust this Meg?"

"With my life."

She gave him a nod of acceptance. "She mentioned Woden's Circle. Is that the ring of stones near Ravenwood?"

"Aye." Lady Nihtscua smiled. "So they endure even in your time?"

"They do. But couldn't I travel back to the future atop Woden's Stair?"

Wulfstan shook his head. "The Stair takes one to the past. The Circle will bring you to the future."

She nodded slowly, absorbing the information. "Who is Sir Robert?"

Grinning, he exchanged glances with his wife. "Lord Ravenwood's brother."

And someone of whom they were both fond, from their expressions. "Apparently, Lord Seacrest's brother too. And Lady Constance?"

"Sir Robert's wife, and my sister." Jocelyn began to pace, and the skirt of her yellow gown swished around her fleet steps. "Druid's Head at daybreak. There's much to do." She glanced at Ardyth. "You'll wear my clothes, of course, and take much of my wardrobe with you."

Ardyth gaped at her. "No. I cannot possibly…"

"You can, and you shall." Jocelyn paused and gave her a sly grin. "'Tis a good excuse to have new garments sewn for *me*."

With an arched eyebrow, Wulfstan regarded her.

"Indeed."

"But first, supper." Freya rubbed her belly. "I'm famished."

Ardyth's first medieval meal was simple but tasty: braised beef and mushrooms in wine sauce, rolls, cherry pottage, and blackberry wine. A flurry of preparation for the impending journey followed. Jocelyn was beyond generous with clothing and other essentials, including two beautifully carved, double-sided bone combs. A kind, middle-aged woman named Edith helped with the packing, and Harold—a manservant with salt-and-pepper hair and thumbs tucked onto his leather belt—watched from the doorway, waiting to send the trunks on their way to Druid's Head that evening. In medieval times and modern, northern England's summers offered extended daylight hours in which to get things done.

Ardyth couldn't help comparing the toiletries the airline had lost only that morning with those Edith arranged now. Rough linen cloths, a paste of ground sage and salt, toothpicks, and mint wine mouthwash weren't ideal for oral hygiene, but they were better than nothing.

Her first trip to the garderobe was nicer than expected. Sweet-smelling herbs mitigated other odors, and she had a choice of either cloths or absorbent sphagnum moss as "toilet paper." Afterward, Jocelyn pulled her aside to explain the same moss served as filling for sanitary napkins held in place by cords and a thin belt during menstruation.

By the time she sank onto Freya's feather-stuffed bed—for the girl had insisted they share it—her body craved sleep. Her mind, however, had other ideas.

Will I be in the twelfth century when I wake tomorrow? This could still be a dream.

"'Tisn't a dream." Freya's high-pitched voice sounded calm, and she followed up her statement with a yawn.

Ardyth turned to her. The mellow evening light streamed in through the open window, illuminating the girl's cherubic face. "Did you just read my thoughts?"

Her yawn ended with a sigh. "I suppose so. It happens sometimes." She rolled over and met Ardyth's gaze. "You are of our line, and presumably of Ravenwood's as well. Have you a similar gift?"

"Well…there's something about my voice. I don't know what exactly, but whenever I give a speech or tell a story out loud, people seem spellbound." It was true. She hoped it would give her an edge when it came time to defend her dissertation. "And when I sing, anyone around me who's hurt heals faster."

"How wonderful!"

"I first realized it when I was seven. My mother twisted her ankle, and when I sang to her, she said she felt tingling right at the sight of the injury. It reduced the swelling and her pain considerably."

Freya turned onto her back again and stared up at the bed's high canopy. "The magic of the voice, weaving around all who hear it. A precious gift indeed." Again, she yawned. "I'm so tired. It's been an eventful day."

That's the understatement of the year! "It has. Sleep now, Freya."

"And you, Ardyth…will you sleep?"

"I'll try."

In the end, slumber favored her, but morning

arrived with all haste. Hasty, too, was her departure amid a chorus of fare-thee-wells from Jocelyn, Freya, and Edith. At her side rode Wulfstan, looking lordly in a royal blue cloak and not unlike Prince Charming atop his white stallion.

There was nothing of the fairytale about *her* appearance. Yes, she wore an embroidered, russet gown, and her hair trailed down her back in one long, thick braid. But she rode astride her brown palfrey, not at all like the princesses in storybooks. She'd asked Jocelyn if she should "ride aside" as if on a sidesaddle. With a dismissive gesture, the lady informed her that most women traveling long distances on horseback rode astride, unless someone else led their mount.

The ten miles to Druid's Head passed quickly, and Ardyth satisfied Wulfstan's curiosity about the twentieth century as best she could. At the first sight of the motte-and-bailey castle, a thrill ran through her. As with Nihtscua, the opportunity to see living, breathing history in place of a ruin was priceless. They passed through the wooden gatehouse, and her gaze darted here and there, taking in the many buildings within the palisade-protected courtyard. She longed to climb the steps to the top of the high mound and explore the small keep, but there wasn't even time to dismount.

A veiled Lady Constance welcomed them with amber eyes that sparkled. She mounted her horse, apologized for their rushed departure, and assured Ardyth her trunks had been added to the baggage cart. Said cart was tended by her husband's towheaded squire, Guy, and her brown-haired handmaiden, Alice, both of whom would also travel to Seacrest.

"My lady," the two intoned as one.

Ardyth smiled at them but wondered if she'd ever get used to being addressed as a noblewoman. At any rate, her luggage seemed in good hands. *If only the airline had been so efficient!*

A tall, broad-shouldered man who could only be Sir Robert bounded down the motte steps. His gray mantle billowed behind him, then swirled around his athletic frame as he swung onto the back of his horse.

After a hurried introduction, he flashed Ardyth a grin that produced dimples on either side of it. With his black hair, gray eyes, and well-chiseled features, he bore a striking resemblance to Professor Seacrest.

I'll have to tell Henri that, she thought. *If I ever see him again...if I actually make it back to my own time. That Meg woman had better be right!*

Wulfstan gave the knight a serious look. "Take care of her, Robert." Then he turned to his descendant. "If ever you have need of me..."

Ardyth nodded. "I'll send word."

His ice blue eyes held her gaze a moment longer. "See that you do." He took his leave, exited through the gatehouse, and struck off toward the North.

Sir Robert grinned at Ardyth, and then his wife. "Well, my ladies...our journey begins."

Kind, courteous, and full of entertaining stories, the knight, his lady, the squire, and handmaiden made wonderful traveling companions. They rode south for three days, stopping two nights: first, at Saint Bartholomew's Nunnery in Newcastle-upon-Tyne, where Lady Constance had been a postulant before her marriage to Sir Robert; second, at an inn in Mydilsburgh (modern Middlesbrough). On the third and final day, they passed through Whitby. Ardyth smiled to herself as she recalled previous research. Before the Viking raids, the town was the site of Streaneshalch, an important Anglo-Saxon double monastery. By this period, there was a new monastery established by Reinfrid, one of William the Conqueror's soldiers who became a monk. Roughly eight centuries later, Whitby would play a role in one of her favorite novels, Bram Stoker's *Dracula*.

And here I am, she thought. *Smack-dab in the middle of its history.*

In the early afternoon, the small party finally arrived at their destination. Ardyth had seen Ravenwood Castle from a distance as they journeyed south, and while it was remarkable, Seacrest was even more so. Built on a high cliff overlooking the sea, the keep was massive, rising four stories above the basement level, with crenellated towers at every corner. Both keep and curtain wall gleamed white in the sunlight. There were two gatehouses: a larger one in front, with a wide, well-trodden road leading into the heart of the sprawling village; a smaller one toward the back left of the castle, with a path leading down to the shore. Sir Robert led them through the front gate and into the spacious courtyard.

Ardyth took a deep breath. *Okay. Time to gird my loins for more introductions. Will they buy our story?*

No sooner had they dismounted than three women emerged from the keep's forebuilding and hastened down the broad steps toward them. The head of the trio was a veiled, middle-aged woman whose beauty and grace were undeniable. Behind her were two younger ladies, pretty and poised, with brown, braided hair, blue eyes, and similarity of features. Sisters?

Sir Robert made a sound that might've been a hiccup.

"What is it?" Lady Constance murmured.

"I haven't seen them in years." His voice was low. "They're the daughters of one of Mother's friends. I know she's eager for Hugh to wed, but..."

"Robert!" The older woman, presumably his mother, rushed forward and clasped his hands. Then she looked from Ardyth to Constance. "And...*two* ladies?"

She smiled warmly at Constance, whose veil gave away that *she* was the new daughter-in-law. Then she dropped her son's hands and turned to study the uninvited guest.

Ardyth's mouth went dry. Now she knew where Sir Robert got his penetrating, gray eyes, for his mother's keen gaze seemed to dive straight into her soul.

The knight placed a hand on Constance's back. "Lady Seacrest, may I present—"

"Robert!" A man in blue raced down the steps and strode toward them.

Ardyth gasped as he took his place beside Lady Seacrest. *That's Hugh?*

Yet another pair of gray eyes adorned his face, but these were familiar. His shining, black hair reached his shoulders, and his clothes were medieval. Other than that, he looked exactly like Henri!

****

Hugh grinned at Robert. "Good to see you again, Brother." He glanced at the veiled lady standing close to Robert's side. She must be his bride. "Prithee, introductions!"

Robert cleared his throat. "I'll start afresh. Lord Seacrest, Lady Seacrest, may I present Lady

Constance?" He turned to Ardyth. "And this is Lord Nihtscua's kinswoman, Lady Ardyth."

For the first time, Hugh focused on the other woman, who was presumably Saxon like her kinsman. Her blonde hair glistened in the sunlight, and her eyes…

They were wide with shock…and something else. Recognition? *Absurd!* Then why did she stare thus?

Robert continued the introductions. "Lady Constance, Lady Ardyth, this is Lord Seacrest and Lady Seacrest." He gestured to the sisters hovering in the background. "And if I'm not mistaken, this is Lady Isobel and Lady Juliana."

Lady Seacrest nodded. "You are correct. They are staying with us for a time."

Hugh sighed in silence. *Of course they are, and I know why.* Robert gave him a meaningful look, which he promptly returned.

Their mother reached a hand toward Constance, and the lady took it. "At last we meet. You're always welcome at Seacrest."

"Indeed," Hugh intoned. "'Tis a pleasure to have you here."

Constance beamed at him, and then his mother. "I thank you. I've so looked forward to this visit."

"As have I." Lady Seacrest released her hand, then regarded Ardyth. "If I may ask, why have *you* come hither?"

The Saxon looked a shade paler as she slid her gaze to his mother. "Lady Margaret of Ravenwood suggested I come."

Lady Seacrest turned to her youngest son. "The lady you call Meg?"

Robert nodded. "Aye, Mother." He smiled at Hugh. "Your search for a scribe is over. Lady Ardyth shall serve you well."

Hugh hesitated, then chuckled. "If you weren't a knight, you'd make a marvelous jester."

Robert sighed. "I see you agree with William on the subject, but I did not speak in jest."

"What? But she cannot—"

"Why not?" the would-be scribe asked. Defiance rang in her voice.

Hugh turned to her. Her face was now flushed, rendering her even more beautiful than before. "It should be obvious to you."

Her brown eyes flared. "Because I'm a woman?"

"Aye. How could you possibly—"

"I can do more than you would ever dream possible."

Aren't you a bold one? "Such as?"

Robert crossed in front of him. Bending toward their mother, he whispered in her ear.

Lady Seacrest raised her eyebrows, then gave the Saxon a look that betokened new interest. "Lady Ardyth, I bid you welcome and look forward to observing your talents. You will share a chamber with Lady Isobel and Lady Juliana." She turned to the sisters. "Pray, show our guest round the keep and to the hall, and thence to your chamber."

Juliana nodded. "Aye, my lady."

Isobel said naught. She looked from Lady Seacrest to Ardyth, then back again. When Juliana motioned for Ardyth to come along, Isobel mutely followed the two ladies through the lower bailey toward the keep.

Ardyth cast no further glance at Hugh, but his gaze

tracked her departure. Within her russet gown, her hips swayed…rather more than he'd seen in other women's gaits.

"And that is that." Lady Seacrest smiled at her sons. "Boys, run along and give me time to acquaint myself with our newest member of the family. Lady Constance?"

Constance flashed Robert a grin, then hastened forward. Shoulder to shoulder, she and their mother strolled toward the gateway to the upper bailey.

Hugh glanced at his brother. "Walk with me." He started across the courtyard.

Robert kept pace with him. "So Mother couldn't resist bringing Lady Isobel and Lady Juliana hither."

"Apparently, *their* mother insisted upon it, but as I'm sure you've guessed, Mother needed little persuasion."

"Indeed. Yet you must admit, she's shown the patience of a saint these many years. Had father lived, he would've arranged a suitable match for you long ago." He sidestepped a pair of chickens. "We all know…curse it, even the chickens know…'tis time you fulfilled your duty."

"To wed." Hugh looked toward the sky, where fluffy white clouds traveled aimlessly and unbound. "And produce heirs."

"Grandchildren. Mother wants them…badly."

"She'll have one soon enough. Isn't Lady Ravenwood near her time?"

Robert nodded. "She is."

"And now you're wed, so another grandchild will soon follow. By the by, Lady Constance is charming. And you look well. Marriage suits you."

"'Twill suit you as well, once you allow it."

Thwunk! The sound of the carpenter's ax cleaving wood punctuated Robert's words.

Hugh's chest tightened, but his stride didn't falter. "I fully intend to marry...when the right lady appears."

"Right, wrong...you're thirty-four. Mother's patience is waning fast."

"No one knows that better than I."

Robert cleared his throat. "Lady Isobel is a comely maid."

"Her sister too."

"But?"

Hugh huffed. "I want what our parents had. A meeting of minds and hearts."

"A rarity, though I was lucky enough to find it."

"As was William." He glanced at the dyer and his apprentice, who carefully turned cloth in a huge vat of red dye.

"Perhaps you'll find it too." A touch of humor threaded Robert's tone.

Hugh stopped short, and a moment later, so did his brother. He studied the knight's face through narrowed eyes. It never failed. The deeper Robert's dimples, the greater the mischief.

"What are you up to?"

"I?" The knight put a hand to his chest and assumed an innocent look that didn't fool Hugh for a moment.

"What did you whisper to Mother?"

"When?"

"You know when."

Robert's grin deepened. "You're right. I do know."

"Well?"

"I cannot say."

"Why not? Did it concern Lady Ardyth?"

Robert shrugged, but his nonchalance seemed forced. "Why should it?"

"Because Mother's demeanor toward her changed directly afterward."

"I suppose it did."

Hugh blew out a long breath. "Robert, you are the most vexing…"

"And the most magnificent brother any man ever had."

"Hmph. Modest, too."

Robert's eyebrows shot up and down. "You may also add loyal and sincere."

"Loyal, aye. But I have cause to question your sincerity."

"How now?"

"Female scribes are scarce, nigh nonexistent. And you just happened to come across one?"

Robert held up his hands. "I've been assured of her skills."

"By whom?"

"Lady Ravenwood's kinswoman, Meg. She said Lady Ardyth is exactly what you've been waiting for."

"Oh?" Hugh arched an eyebrow. "We'll see about that."

Chapter Three

With Isobel and Juliana watching her every move, Ardyth looked around the chamber they would share. It was a modest space at the upper end of the great hall, beyond the dais and behind a decorative wooden partition, but big enough for their travel trunks and two feather mattresses—one large and one small—on the rush-covered floor. Painted flowers and curly-branched trees brightened the back wall.

Knowing what she did about medieval history, she was grateful to have any privacy at all. And a feather mattress in here was better than a straw pallet out in the hall, where a large number of the castle's inhabitants would undoubtedly sleep come nightfall. Of course, the smaller mattress that would be hers was closest to the doorless archway, so she would hear every bump, shuffle, and after-hours chat which occurred. Sleep might be a challenge.

"Have you truly the skill of a scribe?" Juliana's voice was soft; her tone, incredulous.

Ardyth sighed inwardly. There *were* female scribes in the medieval period, though the surviving evidence suggested they were rare. She turned to Juliana. "Noblewomen write, don't they? 'Tis only a step further to write with beauty and garnish with illumination." *Basic illumination, that is. If only I'd learned more!*

"But how? From whom did you learn?"

"My father." It wasn't a lie. Her dad had taught one of the summer courses she'd taken, and he'd encouraged her to read and write when she was still a toddler.

Isobel raised her eyebrows. "Your father?"

Her voice was stronger than her sister's. Maybe she was the older of the two.

Ardyth nodded. "When I was younger, he called me his 'little owl.' "

Isobel's blue eyes narrowed. "Owl…"

Oh, crap! Too late, she remembered at this point in British history, owls weren't symbols of wisdom and learning, but of darkness, impurity, and ill omens.

"He meant nothing bad by it. Owls are night creatures, and I've always loved the night. And unless I'm very tired, it takes me a while to fall asleep, so—"

"Odd," a deep voice interjected.

Ardyth turned to the archway. Hugh filled it, the lord of his domain passing judgment on her with a single word. "Eavesdropping, are you?"

Behind her, one of the girls gasped. At what? Her honest question? His unexpected appearance?

His face betrayed no emotion. He'd been far more expressive outside in the bailey. "Only for a moment."

"Did that moment include the mention of owls?"

He answered with a single nod of his head.

Aren't you a Chatty Cathy? "And?"

"And what?"

"What have you to say about it?"

The slightest twitch of one eyebrow showed…what? Amusement? Annoyance? It was hard to tell.

"Did your father often flout convention?" he asked, stepping into the room.

"By your standards, aye."

"*My* standards?"

Medieval standards, but I can't tell you *that. Man, I need to be more careful about what I say!* "Saxons and Normans view many things differently."

"True." The silver-gray thread of the embroidered design around his collar brought out the color of his eyes, which neither blinked nor averted their gaze from hers.

All at once, the air felt hot and close. "I would step outside…in the bailey. I need fresh air." She started forward, veering to the right to go around him. Then she stopped short beside him and forced herself to say the words all three of them must expect from her. "By your leave."

He turned to face her. "I'll accompany you."

"Why?"

He raised his eyebrows in a show of more emotion than she'd seen since he scoffed at the idea of her as a scribe.

"Why indeed?" Isobel asked. "My lord, I thought you and I were to go hawking."

"Later, my lady." His glance moved from Isobel to Ardyth. Then he motioned toward the archway. "After you."

Although Hugh had spoken the words in Anglo-Norman, their meaning and the rich timbre of his voice so evoked Henri that she hesitated.

"Lady Ardyth?" Puzzlement laced his tone.

She shook off the silly comparison and stepped through the archway and into the hall. The great chamber was even more impressive than Nihtscua's hall. The plastered walls were painted and hung with fine tapestries. Bright banners added color to the high, vaulted ceiling, and there were two massive fireplaces, one on either side of the rows of trestle tables. Most notable was the number of servants. They bustled about cleaning, replacing floor rushes, and casting hooded glances at her and Lord Seacrest, who'd come up beside her. A few servants peeked down from the gallery, which ran all the way around the hall on the floor above.

Hugh cleared his throat. "We'll walk to the upper bailey."

"Why?"

"Do you always ask 'why'?"

She kept pace with his long, confident strides. "There's nothing wrong with curiosity. It implies a nimble mind."

"Then yours is as nimble as they come."

"Why, thank you."

He gave her a look then: a half-smile tamed by a furrowed brow which seemed a blend of humor and confusion. In silence, they exited the hall through a different archway from the one she'd entered. They passed what appeared to be the pantry and buttery, presumably attached to the kitchens; not one of these was part of the brief tour Isobel and Juliana had given her, but why would they be? Such spaces were mostly the domain of servants.

After a short distance, they came to a door which led outside to a wide wooden landing and stairs that hugged the keep and ran down to the upper bailey. She scanned the area as they descended the steps.

Ahead, a tall stone wall spanned the distance between the keep and curtain wall; its central archway must lead to the lower bailey. An abundance of wooden outbuildings lined both this inner wall and the fortified curtain wall. Around to the left—where another stone wall connected the keep to the back left corner of the bailey—stood the postern gate. Beyond that gate, as Robert had explained upon their arrival, a path led down to the shore. The salty air and the cries of seagulls and muffled, crashing waves left no doubt the ocean lay far below them. But high atop the cliff, within this upper bailey, the garden reigned supreme.

A masterpiece of intersecting paths, grass, and beds of herbs, vegetables, and flowers filled the large, square patch of ground. She recognized many of the plants: cumin, fennel, mint, rosemary, rue, sage, coriander, dill, cabbages, leeks, onions, garlic, lilies, poppies, and roses of white, red, and three shades of pink.

As they stepped onto the ground, Hugh made a sweeping gesture with his arms. "This serves as both a physic garden and kitchen garden."

"'Tis wonderful. My mother would love it."

"She knows something of plants?"

"She does." An avid gardener, her mother was always tending one thing or another.

"And your father…how did he learn the skills of a scribe?

Think fast! "When he was younger, he often visited his uncle in the monastery's scriptorium."

"Which monastery?"

Hell if I know! How about the None-of-Your-Business Monastery? She sighed. "May we talk of something else?"

His gray eyes narrowed. "Why?"

"Now you're the one who's curious. And doubtful."

"Can you blame me?"

"No, but I'm tired and don't feel like proving myself at the moment."

She was forever proving herself, in one way or another. Even in the modern world. Her natural hair color had often led to jokes about "dizzy blondes" among her male acquaintances. And while the head of the medieval studies program respected her father, he sided with her ex-boyfriend when John took credit for *her* ideas.

"Judas John," as one of her friends had called him, stole her research and presented it as his own. When she confronted him about it, he gave her a patronizing hug and said he'd done her a favor, that she would've made a fool of herself trying to prove her theory. Of course, it was edgy enough for *him* to espouse without issue. And he'd twisted the truth in such a way that the department head viewed *her* as the academic thief. The doubt and false accusation stung even now, six months after the incident.

"My lady?"

She blinked and brought her senses back to the present, and the handsome, frowning lord beside her. It was uncanny. His descendant, Henri, had to be some kind of genetic doppelganger. But there was a key difference between them: sight unseen, Henri accepted her abilities, trusting her *curriculum vitae* without a shred of doubt; Hugh needed proof. *Different times, for sure.*

Hugh's face and shoulders visibly relaxed.

"You've had a long journey, so I shan't press you today. But I'll see proof of your skills on the morrow, after court."

Right, she thought. A manorial court, probably held in the great hall. "Certainly."

A squeak sounded above, followed by a thud. Turning, she lifted her gaze to the landing. Isobel and Juliana hastened down the wooden stairs toward them.

"My lord," said Isobel, "if we're to go hawking…"

"We must leave anon," he finished for her.

"Aye."

Juliana cleared her throat. "Lady Ardyth, I would speak with you."

Ardyth looked from one sister to the other. *Cleverly done, girls.* Isobel's designs on Hugh were obvious, to another woman at least. "Of course." She glanced at Hugh. "Have I leave to—"

"You have it." He waved her away as Isobel sidled into the narrow space between them.

Juliana motioned for Ardyth to follow her up the stairs. Side by side, they began the climb, as Hugh and Isobel headed for the entrance to the lower bailey.

"My sister is quite determined," Juliana remarked.

Oh, I can see that! "I understand."

Juliana gave her a sidelong glance. "I wonder if you do. Once she's set her mind to a thing, she finds a way to get it."

"An admirable trait."

"I suppose so." She paused when they reached the landing and looked out over the extensive garden.

Ardyth followed her gaze. The straight beds of cultivated plants seemed an open-aired temple to nature's beauty and precision. "You wanted to tell me something?"

"I *was* telling you something."

Ardyth turned to her. "Oh. So you were."

"And one thing more, if I may." Sunlight flickered in her blue eyes and illumined ginger highlights in her tightly coiffed brown hair. Her cheeks were fuller than Isobel's, and she had a slight double chin. Other than those distinctions, the sisters could've been twins.

"Go on."

"I mean no disrespect, but...Lord and Lady Seacrest don't tolerate deceit. 'Tis well and good to attempt a skill, but trickier to master it. Are you sure you can perform the tasks of a scribe?"

Ardyth's stomach lurched. *Well, I was until about two seconds ago.* "I'm sure."

Juliana turned back to the railing. Placing her palms atop it, she surveyed the thriving plot below. "For your sake, I hope so."

****

Seated between Isobel and his mother at the high table in the hall, Hugh relished a bite of strawberry tart and turned his attention to Giles, who'd been a minstrel at Seacrest for more than thirty years. From his position in the wraparound gallery, the gray-haired musician strummed his harp and began to sing.

'Twas a new tune, though the subject matter was old. A treasure beyond measure, hidden in the sea cave beneath the castle. Or so the story went. Whispered around the hearths of nobles and commoners alike, rumors of the Seacrest treasure had existed since before Hugh was born.

Giles's lyrics embellished the tale, painting a melodic picture of phantom lights floating and flitting along the cliffside near the top of the cave. "No mortal would hang from those heights. Are they fairies? Ghosts? No one knows, but many are the seamen aboard their vessels who've seen them." He fell silent, and the strains of his harp took over.

To Hugh's left, Isobel huffed. "What nonsense is this?" Her voice was riddled with irritation.

'Twas only to be expected. Her enthusiasm over their hawking excursion had died a sudden death when a rainstorm cut the outing short.

"Of course, I've heard of the treasure," she continued.

"Who hasn't?" The question came from Juliana, seated to her sister's left.

Isobel gave her a nod, then turned back to Hugh. "But fairy lights along the cliffs? Hogwash."

He shrugged as a cupbearer refilled his wine. "I suppose Giles is trying to compete with Ranulf's more imaginative songs."

To his immediate right, Lady Seacrest sat forward. "I expect you're right, but Giles shouldn't feel threatened. He'll always have a place here. And goliards are expected to perform more provocative fare."

Lady Constance, to his mother's right, leaned toward them. "Did I hear mention of a goliard? I've longed to hear one perform. Is yours a cleric?"

Hugh smiled. "More a wandering scholar, though a wanderer no more now that Lady Seacrest has given him a place here. Ranulf's interests run toward poetry and song, not religion. His satires of the Church make that clear, but he was educated in theology."

Beside Constance, Robert grinned. "What else is a

younger son to do? Other than work toward knighthood, as William and I did."

A long-buried ache resurfaced and tugged at Hugh's heart. He dismissed it and looked to their mother.

She nodded. "Thankfully, knighthood suits you both, though it has given my nerves a beating on several occasions."

"I imagine it has." Constance looked at Robert—whose dimples deepened considerably—then back at Lady Seacrest. "So Ranulf is a younger son. Of whom?"

"Lord Harcourt, one of my late husband's oldest friends. When Ranulf came calling, I thought it only right to offer him a position here."

Robert gestured toward the musicians. "Giles has finished. 'Tis Ranulf's turn."

The goliard laid his rebec against his shoulder and lifted the bow. Lively music streamed forth.

Robert reached for Constance's hand, and his head bobbed from side to side in time with the rhythm. Just beyond him, the feisty Saxon "scribe" beamed at the young musician. She'd changed into a gown of forest green, and the color suited her, as did her glowing countenance. Ranulf's pleasant voice and clever words seemed the source of her delight. In fact, his music—together with his rakish grin and dark hair and eyes—had turned every female head in the hall. Lady Ardyth wasn't the first maiden to succumb to the goliard's charm, and she wouldn't be the last.

Not my concern, Hugh thought.

But the idea gnawed at him and continued to do so even when he and his family retired to the solar after supper. Sipping spiced wine, he and Robert lounged in cushioned, high-backed chairs before the lifeless hearth. Their mother and Lady Constance engaged in a spirited game of Fox and Geese at a table beneath the open window.

"What ails you, Brother?" Robert's penetrating gaze sparkled with barely contained intensity.

Hugh sighed inside. "Not a thing." He lifted his cup and took a swig. Cinnamon, cardamom, ginger, and nutmeg danced upon his tongue.

"I couldn't help but notice…"

"What?"

"Your gaze sought Lady Ardyth quite a bit this evening."

"Not overmuch. Anyway, what does it matter? *Her* gaze was fixed on Ranulf."

Robert's dimples appeared. "Was it? And how would you know that if you weren't watching?"

"Point taken." Hugh took another sip of wine.

"No one could blame her for staring," Constance remarked.

"No indeed," Lady Seacrest agreed. "I've known many a sorrier sight than the cleft of Ranulf's chin."

"His chin?" Hugh glanced at her over his shoulder. "Is that what enthralls every female in Christendom?"

"'Tis more than that, I'll wager." Robert snickered into his cup.

Hugh turned back to his brother. "Laugh all you want. I shan't see our guest abused."

Robert's eyes widened. "Oh, is *that* it? You're worried he'll seduce her?"

"Not worried. But not at ease either."

"Relax. Lady Ardyth is a sensible woman, and

unless things have changed since my last visit, Ranulf cares more for his music than for those who admire his...er, chin. I must say, his skill with the rebec is exceptional. William and I encountered the instrument on several occasions in the Holy Land, though 'twas always played upright on the lap. Ranulf is as good as any musician we heard there...perhaps better."

"I don't doubt it."

"But you *do* doubt his intentions toward..."

"Forget it, Robert."

The knight looked over his shoulder, trading glances with their mother.

"I saw that," Hugh admonished them.

Lady Seacrest gave him a smile that appeared innocent on the surface, yet highly suspicious. "Cannot a mother and son exchange looks of amusement?"

Hugh frowned. They shared more than amusement. 'Twas solidarity he sensed between them. And if his steadfast mother and mischievous brother agreed on something, it meant only one thing: trouble.

Chapter Four

Night spread its wings over Seacrest, and Ardyth eyed her feather mattress with a silent sigh. It was better than the straw mattresses on which she'd slept during the trip here. But combined with the constant rumbles and murmurs drifting in from the hall, it could make for a long night ahead. With any luck, she'd adapt quickly.

Juliana placed an oil lamp on the small table between the two "beds." "Ranulf sang with feeling, didn't he?"

With arms crossed, Isobel stood in the archway. "That he did." She shifted her gaze to Ardyth. "Despite your preference for the night, I trust you'll sleep well. You had a long journey."

Ardyth nodded. "I did, and I hope you're right. 'Tis a pity the rain stopped, for the sound of it might've helped. Though I'm sorry it prevented you from hawking longer."

Isobel's eyes narrowed. "Why should you be sorry?"

It's called empathy. "I know you were looking forward to it."

"She certainly was." Flipping her brown braid over her shoulder, Juliana crossed to a trunk along the wall, opened it, and reached inside. "Take heart, Isobel. At least you had *some* time with Lord Seacrest."

"Precious little," Isobel grumbled. She shuffled over to her sister. "What are you looking for?"

"My comb." With furrowed brow, Juliana rearranged the trunk's contents. "I'm certain I put it here this morning."

Ardyth hurried to her smaller chest and pulled out one of her combs. As far as she could tell, her roommates were well-groomed, so why not share one? If lice entered the picture, she'd find a way to disinfect the instrument. "You may borrow mine, if you like."

As one, the sisters turned. They stared at her as if she had two heads.

Let's try this again. "I have two, so you're welcome to use one."

"In sooth?" Juliana asked.

Ardyth nodded and handed her the comb.

Juliana examined it closely and ran her finger along the decorative engraving. "'Tis very fine."

"'Twas a gift."

Isobel's mouth twitched. "From whom?"

"My kinsman's wife, Lady Nihtscua."

A cry rang out in the hall. Then a child began to sob.

Ardyth hastened out of the chamber and into the hall. Following the doleful sound to the midpoint of the right wall, she came to a twenty-something, veiled woman and a boy with curly brown hair no more than seven or eight years old. Lying on the floor and gripping his bandaged arm, the boy wept while the woman crouched at his side, tenderly stroking his sweat-beaded brow.

Ardyth's heart ached as she knelt beside the boy. "Are you in pain?"

Tears streamed down his face, but he found the strength to nod in answer.

"He burned himself in the kitchens today," the woman explained. "The pain is that bad, I don't know how I'll get him to sleep."

"What's his name?"

"Corbin, my lady. He's my son."

"And your name?"

"Millicent."

Ardyth bit her lip. She didn't relish the idea of calling attention to herself, but she had to help. "May I sing to him?"

Millicent blinked. "Sing?"

"Something soothing to take his mind off the pain."

"If you think 'twill help…"

Based on past experience, Ardyth knew it would. But what to sing? A tune from *The Wizard of Oz* popped into her mind. These people wouldn't understand the lyrics, and the song's structure was quite different from anything they would've heard. But "Somewhere Over the Rainbow" would have to do.

She started to sing. Slowly, Corbin's brow smoothed. He stopped crying, released his arm, and watched her face intently. By the time she reached the song's bridge, the ambient noise in the hall had ceased, and many of the people, including Ranulf and Giles, had gathered around them. All eyes were on her.

She should be used to such attention; it found her every single time she sang or told a story. Even so, it unnerved her. But if her voice lessened people's burdens—physical or otherwise—she would use it.

When at last she fell silent, Corbin smiled. "My arm…it feels a lot better."

Millicent ran her fingers through his hair. "It does? God be praised. And...my hip feels better too." She regarded Ardyth with soft eyes that glowed with gratitude. "You have the most beautiful voice."

"She has indeed." Ranulf grinned, his gaze holding Ardyth's. He was an attractive guy with his dark hair and eyes, and if his smooth skin were any indication, he was her age or slightly younger. "My lady...Ardyth, is it?"

"Aye."

"Your talent borders on...how shall I say this? Angelic."

Beside him, Giles grunted. "But she cannot be a trained musician."

Ranulf threw the minstrel an impatient look. "Does it matter? Her song was enchanting." He returned his focus to her. "I couldn't understand the words, though. What language was it?"

"A variant of the Saxon tongue." It was true. Modern English was a direct descendant of Anglo-Saxon.

"I don't speak it myself, but I thought I heard a Saxon flair. The music itself...the phrasing...'twas quite unique."

"Actually, I found *your* songs unique."

Giles rolled his eyes, and a strand of gray hair fell over the left one. He puckered his lips and blew the offending hair back into place. With a sour expression, he stalked off toward the opposite side of the hall.

Ranulf sighed. "Don't mind him. I trow he's jealous of your natural abilities, as he seems to be of mine."

"He shouldn't be. He's a wonderful musician

himself." She turned to Corbin, who watched her still. "I'll leave you to sleep now."

He smiled through a yawn. "Thank you."

"Aye, my lady." Unshed tears shone in his mother's eyes. "We're most grateful for your help."

Ardyth's heart swelled. "'Twas my pleasure, Millicent. Truly." Standing, she regarded Ranulf. "I should go to my bed too."

"So soon?" He strolled alongside her.

She looked toward her bedchamber, still some distance away. The sisters stood just outside the archway, observing her and Ranulf. Isobel frowned and disappeared into the chamber. Juliana's face was serene. She hesitated on the threshold, then followed her sister inside. Both were abed with eyes closed by the time Ardyth entered. Apparently, they were done talking.

****

Late morning of the next day, Hugh awaited Ardyth in the solar with hands clasped behind his back. All was in readiness: the angled writing desk, prepared parchment, quill pen, inkwell, and knife. Even the sun obliged him, rendering the space as bright as any scriptorium could hope to be.

He tapped his foot. *Where is she? How long must I wait?*

In a flurry of fine blue cloth, she appeared in the doorway. Smoothing the skirt of her gown, she slowed her steps and entered the solar. Her cheeks were pink; her breathing, fast. She'd come in a hurry.

He motioned to the stool in front of the desk. "Prithee, sit. I'm eager to see your work."

"Evidently." With a droll smile, she sat down.

Pert as ever, he thought, suppressing a grin.

She looked up at him, and the sunlight awakened flecks of gold in her eyes. "I thought, if you approve, that I would write in the Norman language."

He took a step back. "I assumed you'd write in Latin."

She shrugged. "I could, but wouldn't you prefer to read your family's history in your own tongue?"

"I suppose so. Very well, then."

She beamed up at him with remarkably straight teeth. "What shall I write to prove myself to you? Our names? A poem?"

He thought for a moment, seeking an answer.

Her lips twisted. "The Magna Carta?" Humor touched her words.

"The great charter? Of which charter do you speak?"

"Um, nothing." Her expression was enigmatic. "Forgive me. I jest when I'm nervous."

"Why should you be nervous? Unless you cannot write as—"

"I can write well enough. Why don't we start with your parents? What are their given names?"

"Simon and Lillian."

She dipped the pen into the ink and inscribed the names in skillful, fluid strokes. Her style was beautiful, neat, and easy to read.

Impressive. "Good," he said aloud.

Again, she smiled. "I'm glad you approve. What next?"

"Write my words as I say them. Are you ready?"

"I am." She poised the pen above the parchment.

He gave her a nod. "My family…"

50

She began to write.

"…originated in Normandy," he continued, "a fertile land…settled by the Northmen of old."

When she finished writing, she looked up at him. Her eyes twinkled. "I love history!"

The passion and delight in her voice caught him off guard. He cleared his throat. "As do I. 'Tis why I want my family's history in writing, preserved for future generations."

"A noble aim." She tilted her head to the side and gave him an impish grin. "Of course, in order to *have* future generations, you'll need heirs."

He stiffened. "I know that."

"There must've been countless possibilities over the years…suitable matches that would've increased your fortune. Yet here you stand, alone and…how old?"

"Thirty-four. How old are *you*?"

"Twenty-five."

He folded his arms. "Why haven't *you* married? Mayhap your forthright manner has—"

"I'm proud of my manner!" She dropped her pen and leapt to her feet. "And of my intelligence. I'll defy anyone who belittles them."

"That I believe."

She stepped closer and lifted her chin. "Only the greatest love would persuade me to wed. I've seen such devotion from my parents. They'd die for one another without hesitation. If I marry—and that's a big if—nothing less will do."

His eyes widened. Here was someone who felt exactly as he did on the subject. He'd never expected a man to share his opinion, much less a woman. "Your reason echoes my own."

Her chin lowered slightly. "Oh?"

"My parents shared a great love, and I want the same."

"With Lady Isobel?"

"Perhaps."

'Twould please his mother immensely. Isobel's family as well, and nearly everyone expected the union. The lady was beautiful, graceful, and of noble birth. Most of the time, he enjoyed her company, and he wished her well. Nevertheless, something held him back.

Ardyth stepped backward. "Then I hope you two find happiness together. You're a man ahead of your time, and you deserve the best."

"And you are the most outspoken woman I've ever met. Still, we share a common desire, so I hope you, too, find what you seek."

"Thank you. But honestly, I don't need a man to be happy."

His hands dropped to his sides. "You don't?"

"But I do need a bath."

He burst out laughing. "A bath?"

"Or at the very least, a swim in the ocean."

"You can swim?"

"Like a fish."

He shook his head. "I cannot believe it."

"Why not?" She planted her hands on her hips. "Oh, wait…let me guess. Because I'm a woman."

"'Tis highly improbable—"

"I tell you now, I can do anything a man can do."

He raised his eyebrows. "Anything?"

She made a face. "Well, not everything, but most things."

"Including swimming." He couldn't temper the doubt in his tone.

Once more, she lifted her chin. "Aye. I've proven my skills as a scribe, haven't I?"

"You have."

"Then lead me to the water."

He gazed into her blunt brown eyes for a long moment. She was serious. "Very well. This I must see."

Chapter Five

With a neatly folded replacement chemise in hand, Ardyth followed Hugh along one of the narrower garden paths toward the upper bailey's postern gate. He'd said his customary "after you," but she'd told him to lead on; he knew the way better than she. His shoulders—richly clad in a teal tunic—looked even broader from behind. His shoulder-length black hair glistened in the sun.

Too handsome for your own good, she thought. *Just like Henri.* And Robert, for that matter, though he seemed to have found his bliss with Constance. Their brother William she hadn't met, but if the family genes ran true to form, Lord Ravenwood must be drop dead gorgeous.

"Lady Ardyth!" a high-pitched voice chimed from a distance behind her.

She stopped and turned. "Corbin!" Her heart swelled as the injured boy from the night before dropped his basket into a patch of herbs and scampered toward her. "I didn't see you. Where were you hiding?"

He grinned, and his dark hair appeared even more unruly than she remembered. "Nowhere. I just came out to fetch rosemary and dill for Aubert."

"Aubert?"

"The head cook," Hugh said at her back.

Corbin nodded and laid a hand on his bandaged

54

arm. "It still aches, but 'tis much better. Will you sing to me again tonight?"

"Sing?" Hugh asked.

The boy smiled. "Aye. I burned my arm yesterday, and it hurt so bad I couldn't sleep…until her ladyship sang and made it better."

"Did she?" The disbelief in Hugh's tone rang clear.

There was no way to explain her gift to someone who hadn't experienced it firsthand. The blasted man doubted even her ability to swim; if she hit him with a vocal gift that bordered on magic, he'd laugh her all the way back to Northumberland.

"I did." She cleared her throat. "In the hall last night."

Corbin bobbed his head. "Then a lot of the pain went away. My mother's hip felt better, too." He scratched his nose, smudging it with dirt, and gave her a pleading look. "Won't you sing tonight?"

Smiling, she shrugged. "Aye, if it means that much to you."

"And maybe you could stay and tell me a story, like my father did…when he was alive. My mother does it sometimes, but lately she's been too tired."

How could she say no to that? "Of course."

His eyes alight, Corbin clapped his hands together. "Thank you, my lady." He scurried back to his basket.

She swiveled around but avoided Hugh's gaze. "Shall we continue?"

The path widened as they neared the postern gate, allowing them to walk side by side. A burly gatekeeper with mussed, auburn hair manned this second, smaller gatehouse. He gave her a curious look, then offered Hugh a nod and a gruff, "My lord."

Lord Seacrest returned his nod. "Philippe."

They passed through the gatehouse to the descending, well-trodden path beyond.

"So you can sing," Hugh said, his voice threaded with amusement.

"Everyone can sing."

"But apparently, you sing well."

She shrugged. "Well enough."

"The boy is clearly in awe of you. 'Twas kind of you to agree to the storytelling."

"I help where I can." But what story to tell? The people might be familiar with some aspects of Arthurian legend—which might not agree with her version—so that was out. Maybe science fiction would work, if adapted to the medieval period. *Yes. A long time ago in a land far, far away...*

They continued down to the shore. At the far end of a sizeable beach sat several boats, large and small. The crashing of waves and swelling grandeur of the sea heightened her senses, and she breathed deeply of the salty air.

Veering right, Hugh led her along the coast, which thinned considerably as they rounded the craggy headland atop which the castle perched. In the distance, where the shoreline widened again, was a fishing weir, a timber wall with its attendant netting. Beside her, directly below the upper bailey, yawned a massive sea cave.

She stopped and stared, her mouth agape. The sand-floored hollow had to be at least three hundred feet wide and almost as high. "This must be the cave Giles sang about."

Hugh had halted beside her. "Aye. 'Tis a good

place for you to disrobe…at present, that is. When the tide rises, water covers the base of the cave." He gave her a sidewise look. "Do you still intend to strip down to your chemise…in front of me…and wade in the sea?"

"Absolutely. And I'll do more than just wade."

"I'll believe it when I see it."

She lifted her chin. "Wait a moment, and you shall."

With firm strides, she entered the cave, and he followed. Roughly twenty yards ahead and twenty feet high was a ledge, beyond which the ancient sea had carved three tall but narrow openings.

She pointed. "Tunnels?"

He nodded. "Extensive and reported to hide treasure, as Giles reminded everyone last night."

"You sound annoyed."

"He's feeding rumors about something that doesn't exist. Years ago, even before my birth, there was a shipwreck." He cocked his head toward the ocean. "Just out there. My father and his men rescued the survivors and saved much of the vessel's load before the sea could claim it."

"But there was no gold or silver aboard?"

He shook his head. "Not according to my father. Nevertheless, the legend was born."

She looked from one tunnel entrance to the next, and then the next. The ledge in front of them was substantial. It ran along the rock wall to the right, all the way to the mouth of the cave, winding around it to continue along the outer cliff.

Again, she pointed. "Where does that lead?"

"Shouldn't you be doffing your clothes?"

Her eyes narrowed. "In other words, you don't intend to answer my question."

He grinned. "Clever, aren't you?"

She returned his smile. "I like to think so."

"If you're stalling because you cannot swim…"

"Oh, I can swim." She could hardly wait to feel the cool water on her skin.

He folded his arms, and his intense, gray eyes held a dare. "Then show me."

"Hold this." She handed him the folded smock. *Get ready to eat crow, buddy!* Quickly, she removed her boots, hose, and tunics. When only her thin, white chemise remained, she stole a peek at her skeptical host. He stared at her bare feet.

She sighed. "I know. My feet are hardly attractive. In fact, I've always thought my toes resemble…"

He raised his eyebrows. "What?"

Astronauts. But I can't tell you that. "Nothing."

His eyebrows settled again, but the orbs beneath them seemed to glow with a new light. "I beg to differ with your opinion. Your feet are quite…lovely."

She almost laughed, until heat flooded her cheeks. *I'm blushing?* "Thank you," she muttered. With an inward groan, she started toward the water. *For crying out loud! He only complimented your feet. Your pale, crazy, NASA-evoking feet. Get a grip!*

The ocean breeze caught the hem of her smock as she stepped into the surf. Foamy water—colder than she would've liked—enveloped her feet. *Thank God for the heat of the sun!* But this was the closest she'd come to a bath in days, and she was determined to prove her skills to the man who underestimated her at every turn. She waded forward, and the brisk, undulating water swallowed her calves, knees, thighs, and hips.

"Lady Ardyth!"

She turned. Her dry smock in his hands, Hugh stood with feet well apart on the wet sand.

"You needn't prove your courage further!" he called above the lapping, swishing voice of the sea. "Come back before—"

"Courage isn't the point! Swimming is!" The level of the surrounding water lowered to her thighs, signaling a coming wave.

She turned just as it crested and dived headfirst into it. Completely submerged in the chill, rushing water, she headed left and allowed herself to rise to the surface. She swam freestyle for several strokes, then flipped onto her back and floated with abandon. After a minute or two, she flipped over, and swam in the opposite direction. Then she stood with the water at her ribs, waited for the next wave, and indulged in bodysurfing, which carried her with a whoosh back toward shore.

Satisfied, she straightened, barely knee deep in the water. Her wet chemise clung to her frame, and she knew Lord Seacrest was getting a lordly eyeful right now. Her nipples were rock-hard from the cold.

She rolled her eyes toward the bright, blue sky. *My kingdom for a bra! And throw in a pair of underwear, too!* But both articles of clothing were back at Nihtscua and not likely to appear anytime soon. For the first time since plunging into the surf, she regarded Hugh.

Eyes wide, her dry smock clutched in his hands, he stood as if frozen. Only his gaze moved, traveling from her breasts to the apex of her thighs.

She pulled the smock away from her flesh as best

she could and advanced toward him, stopping an arm's length away. "I told you I could swim."

He blinked. Then his full, sensual lips curled into a smile. "Indeed, you did."

"And?"

"And what?"

"You've doubted me twice already. Perhaps you owe me an apology."

His eyes widened, then relaxed. "Perhaps I do. Pray…forgive me."

The words couldn't have come easily, and the fact he'd said them made her grin. "I forgive you. This time. But I ask respectfully that you not underestimate me again."

For two seconds, he hesitated. "'Tis a reasonable request, and I shall endeavor to honor it." He gave her a quizzical look. Then he shook his head and chuckled. "Is there anything you cannot do?"

She thought for a moment. "I've never ridden aside. If I'm going to ride something, I spread my legs." The instant the words left her mouth, she cringed inside. *Good God. That came out all wrong!*

Humor curved his lips, but his eyes smoldered. Did his thoughts mirror hers? He took a step closer, and his masculine aura invaded her personal space. "Tell me more."

Though every inch of her skin was wet, her mouth went dry. She licked her lips, which tasted of salt, and almost spoke Modern English, but caught herself just in time. "There's nothing more to say." She cleared her throat. Once. Twice. And then a third time. The phlegm of the world seemed to have congregated in her throat.

His smile remained. "Are you all right?"

Finally, her throat cooperated. "I am. But I must change." She snatched the dry chemise from his hands and strode toward the cave.

He caught up to her and walked by her side. "Few come this way anymore. Most fishermen prefer a path that leads directly down to the weir. All the same, I'll stand watch while you change and escort you back to the keep."

"Thank you, but that won't be necessary."

"Perhaps not, but one cannot be too cautious when—"

"Truly, my lord." She halted at the mouth of the cave and turned to him. "I can take care of myself, and I'm certain you have more important duties to perform."

"I see. You desire privacy."

"Precisely." *And a bit of breathing room.* She hadn't encountered such virility since…well, since Henri. But neither he nor Hugh fit into her carefully plotted future. Her intuition whispered that this visit to medieval England would be brief, and whatever the century, she couldn't risk a man's interference, not after what John pulled.

Hugh shifted his weight from one leg to the other. "You needn't fear I'll take advantage of you."

"I don't. I know you're a man of honor. Even if you weren't…"

"You can take care of yourself, as you said."

"Exactly."

His gaze held hers for a long moment. Then he blinked. "Very well. I look forward to…relating my family's history to you."

"I look forward to writing it."

He gave her a curt nod, turned, and disappeared around the jagged edge of the weathered cliff.

****

As the lifeblood of Seacrest mellowed, each inhabitant setting aside the day's labors, Hugh abandoned the solar and headed for the gallery overlooking the great hall. Robert and Constance had retired for the night, and his mother, he presumed, strolled the quiet baileys, as she often did on a summer's eve when the weather was fine.

He was alone with his thoughts, and one person dominated them: Lady Ardyth.

From the moment they met, she surprised him. Never more so than today. The fluidity of her writing. Her similar desire for love in marriage. The way her eyes lit up when she spoke of history. Her skillful, uninhibited swim in the sea. Her self-reliance, which rivaled even his mother's. The beauty emanating from every part of her, from her golden hair to her tiny toes. And the parts in between...

His manhood hardened at the memory of her drenched chemise and the bounty it revealed. Full breasts. Taut nipples. Curvaceous hips and legs. The shadowy hint of dark blonde hair that hid her feminine mound.

From his fifteenth year on, he'd sampled the pleasures of women, noble and otherwise. Not one of them had the same appeal, the same...*force* as the Saxon lady who was now his scribe.

Right. She's my scribe and nothing more. Her words and actions made that clear; she'd all but ordered him from her presence earlier.

'Twas just as well. Her unconventional ways

were…

A sudden realization interrupted his thoughts. He paused midway up the stairs to the gallery and listened…to nothing. He frowned. The din from the hall should've reached him by now. Yet all was quiet, until…

A woman's voice sounded, sought him where he stood. 'Twas singing, like none he'd heard in all his life. Mellifluous. Clear. Sublime.

He hurried up the remaining steps to the gallery. In a haze of wonder, he advanced toward the railing and peered below.

Perched on a stool in front of the dais, Ardyth sang to the crowd. The boy, Corbin, knelt not two yards from her feet. Some onlookers stood; others sat. All appeared captivated by the lady whose music soared to the highest beams of the hall.

Even Juliana had emerged from behind the wooden screen that demarcated the bedchamber. Isobel was noticeably absent.

His entire body resonated with Ardyth's voice. Every care, every woe faded from his mind. All at once, he understood the healing power of beauty. True beauty, the kind which stirred the soul.

When she fell silent, the people clapped. She gave many of them a nod and a humble, closed-mouth smile. She almost looked embarrassed. Perhaps that explained why she hadn't noticed his presence above her. Had anyone seen him? With such entertainment at hand, he doubted it.

As the applause abated, Corbin leapt to his feet. "And now my story!"

Ranulf, who stood nearby, turned to the lad. "A

story?"

"Aye. She promised to tell one."

"Did she now?"

Sitting on a bench with arms crossed, Giles grunted. "'Tis obvious she did, or he wouldn't have mentioned it."

Ranulf grinned, first at the minstrel, then at Ardyth. "Why don't you tell us *all* a story?"

Giles gaped at him. "Her ladyship is a woman."

"Well spotted," Ranulf quipped.

"Women don't—"

"'Tis highly irregular, I know. But I'll wager her ladyship could weave a delightful tale."

Corbin clapped his hands. "Oh please, my lady!"

Ardyth hesitated for a long moment, then smiled at the boy. "Very well."

Hugh's grip on the wooden railing tightened as he observed the grinning goliard. He didn't like Ranulf's gaze, adhered as with pine sap to Ardyth. The man was too attentive and amiable. Nigh besotted.

Beyond the dais, Juliana hugged the decorative screen and trained *her* gaze on Ranulf. Her face softened as she stared at him.

Hugh raised a hand from the rail and stroked his jaw. *Interesting...*

Ardyth cleared her throat and straightened. A hush fell over the hall, and she began a fanciful tale of a squire named Luc who discovered he had magical powers and joined others—including Bénoni, an aged knight and a brave princess named Lèane—in a desperate fight against evil invaders. The story itself was intriguing, but Ardyth's facial expressions, gestures, honeyed voice, and fervor raised it to the level of enchantment. When at last she finished, thunderous applause filled the hall.

"Do you see something you like?"

Hugh started, then calmly turned. "Mother. How long have you been standing there?"

Her smile was tender. "Long enough to know Lady Ardyth is a gifted storyteller."

"I shan't deny it."

She shrugged as if nonchalant, but her gray eyes twinkled in the torchlight. "Why deny what is right in front of us?"

He frowned. "Whatever do you mean?"

"Naught." Avoiding his gaze, she surveyed the crowd below. "I don't see Lady Isobel."

"Perhaps she went early to bed."

"With such excitement just outside her door?"

"There is no door."

"Quite. I've not asked 'til now, but…how is your relationship with her? Cordial?"

His chest tightened. "I would say so."

"More than with her sister, I presume."

"'Tis true I have less in common with Lady Juliana. Mother…"

"And Lady Ardyth?"

His eyes narrowed. "What about her?"

"Has she proven herself as a scribe?"

"She has."

Her smile was back. He wasn't sure he liked it. Turning toward the hall, he caught a final glimpse of Ardyth as she and Juliana disappeared into their chamber.

He spun back around. "What did Robert say to you when he first arrived?"

Suddenly, his mother's headrail consumed her focus. She adjusted the veil with exaggerated care. "You were there. You heard his words plainly."

"Except for those he whispered in your ear."

"Oh. Aye. He said nothing of consequence."

"Mother, look at me."

Her hands dropped to her sides, and she met his gaze. "Of course, my son."

He sighed. "In my experience, whispers carry great import. But then you know that already. What did he say?"

"I cannot tell you." Her expression was smooth, without emotion.

"Wherefore?"

"Because."

He heaved a louder sigh. "Shall we play this game all night, or will you give me a direct answer?"

"My dearest Hugh, only you have the answer."

"Are you *trying* to vex me?"

"Not at all." She patted his arm. "But I shan't sway your judgment."

"And Robert's words would do that?"

"They might."

He tapped his foot and ran a hand through his hair. They were two of a kind, Robert and his mother. He hadn't fully realized that until now. What secret did they share? Would it affect his future? Or that of Seacrest?

He infused his voice with calm he didn't feel. "Did his words concern Lady Ardyth? Her parentage? Her upbringing? Something in her background which—"

"I told you, I cannot say. And now, I shall retire to my chamber." She laid a hand on his cheek. "Sleep well, son." She whirled around and left him, alone and unsatisfied above the hall.

Chapter Six

Ardyth settled into medieval life easier than expected, and two weeks passed in the blink of an eye. On occasion, she joined Lillian (Lady Seacrest), Constance, Isobel, and Juliana, who busied themselves with embroidery, spinning, and teaching five preteen girls sent to Seacrest from surrounding households how to behave in polite society. The last task Ardyth managed well, and she was getting better at handling the yarn and distaff. But she couldn't sew to save her life. She explained her shortcomings by stressing the amount of practice necessary to become a competent scribe, and as far as she knew, the other women bought the excuse.

From time to time, she popped into the kitchens, bakehouse, granary, brewery, kennel, stables, and various storehouses and workshops in both baileys to study the daily lives of the people. She even visited the mews, where the falconer showed great patience in "weathering" and training Hugh's new peregrine falcon. Ideas for her doctoral dissertation flowed easily; the difficulty would be in choosing only one topic.

In the evenings before bed, the keep's inhabitants gathered in the great hall to hear her sing and tell stories. Entertaining in such a way was a privilege reserved for medieval men, but Hugh and his mother allowed her to do it. She silently thanked her parents for all the musicals they'd made her watch, for they provided a wealth of tunes. For the stories, she created original tales but also adapted several of her favorite books and movies to the medieval period. Most of the audience, including Juliana, seemed to look forward to the nightly ritual. Even the Seacrests had taken to listening from the gallery. Isobel and Giles listened too, often with hostile expressions, but Ranulf praised her performances with gusto.

The bulk of her days she spent writing about Hugh's ancestors in Normandy, ornamenting the script and margins afterward. He'd just begun to tell her of his immediate family and promised stories about his father soon. He seemed pleased with her work and grew handsomer by the day, as if he wasn't hot-as-sin to begin with! On the whole, he treated her as an employee. He was courteous, yet distant; more acquaintance than friend. A remarkable achievement for a medieval man who'd basically seen her naked.

But it was all for the best. One day soon, she'd return to her own time. She only hoped she'd arrive at a date shortly after she'd left. She couldn't bear the thought of her parents agonizing over her disappearance. What Henri had made of it, she couldn't guess.

According to the Ravenwood woman, Meg, she would know when to leave. So far, no such instinct had seized her, and she felt obligated to finish the Seacrest family history. Besides, Meg had stressed she must stay even after Robert and Constance left.

Now, the afternoon before their departure, Ardyth strolled the lower bailey with Constance. She smiled at two young women who were tending partridges and pheasants, then turned to her companion.

"'Tis hard to believe you're leaving on the morrow. I'll miss you and Sir Robert. You've both been so kind and open."

"Open?" Constance cast her a sidewise glance. "Whom do you view as guarded? Lady Isobel?"

A peacock paraded in front of the ox shed. Its iridescent feathers shimmered in the sunlight.

"Aye, but I was thinking of..." Ardyth shook her head. "Never mind. I've no wish to speak ill of anyone."

"I'll warrant I can guess your thoughts. Lady Seacrest. Am I right?"

Ardyth gave her a rueful smile. "How did you know?"

"She's a formidable woman. In sooth, I heard so much about her from my husband and Lord Ravenwood, I was anxious before we arrived."

"You feared her disapproval?"

Constance nodded. "As you do now."

"Her words are kind, but she says very little to me. At times..."

"Go on."

Ardyth sighed. "I catch her watching me."

Constance's mouth twitched. Then she laughed, and the sound was as lovely and delicate as the tinkling of a crystal chandelier. "Lady Seacrest is nothing if not observant. She watches everyone, including me."

"Well, I know she approves of *you*. But how does she feel about me?"

"She admires your work."

"Does she?"

"She told me so."

Ardyth released a long breath. "That's a relief! Actually, I've considered asking her about certain aspects of the family history." As every historian knew, consulting a variety of sources was important.

"I trow her ladyship would welcome your questions."

They passed the pigsty. Ardyth wrinkled her nose and grinned at one of the larger swine. *You and me both,* she thought. She dearly missed antiperspirant and craved a bath. A real one, with warm water that would cradle and soothe every inch of her body.

Not that she didn't bathe. Every morning, servants provided her, Juliana, and Isobel with basins of cold water. Once a week, they also brought jugs of water, so the trio could wash their hair. Of course, everyone washed hands before and after each meal, and Hugh had given her leave to swim in the ocean whenever she wanted…alone. She enjoyed the freedom and solitude, yet there were moments when "alone" felt lonely.

Hugh's face flashed before her mind's eye. Gray eyes smiling. Black hair writhing on the ocean breeze.

So much for my lovely feet, she mused. *If he really found me attractive, he'd join me on the beach.*

"Where are your thoughts?" Constance asked.

Ardyth blinked. They were still walking, well past the pigsty, which was the last thing she recalled seeing. The clangs from the smithy grew louder by the second. "Nowhere that matters."

"Hmm." There was doubt in her tone, followed by a loaded pause.

Ardyth stopped short in front of the tailor's shop. "What do you mean by your 'hmm'?"

Constance halted and regarded her with hands

clasped in front of her torso. "In case you were wondering…Lord Seacrest approves of you."

"Of my work, you mean?"

"Of more than that."

"My stories, then. And my singing."

Constance grinned. "Among other things."

Ardyth's stomach quivered. "You cannot mean…"

"I do."

"He gives no indication of it."

"No? His attention falls on you as much as it does Isobel, perhaps more."

Ardyth's eyes widened, and a strange blend of pleasure and alarm ran through her. "Isobel is better suited to him."

It was true. For starters, they were from the same time. Their families had been acquainted for years, and she understood his world and expectations in a way Ardyth never could. Right this minute, Isobel and Juliana were somewhere in the forest with Hugh, Robert, and the rest of the hunting party. Out of scholarly interest, Ardyth had attended one hunt, and that had been enough for her. She realized it wasn't just sport; how else would they acquire meat for the table? But the sight of a frightened or injured creature— animal or human—was hard to stomach. Isobel, on the other hand, relished the hunt. She was everything a medieval woman should be, and she could embroider up a storm.

Constance stared at her for a long moment. "Are you quite sure of that?"

Ardyth *was* sure, about both Isobel and Hugh. Her relationship with John had been bad enough. A guy with a medieval mentality would be ten times worse!

She belonged in 1986, where her parents and dream career waited.

"I don't need a man," she declared.

"Perhaps not, but do you *want* one?"

"Not particularly."

Constance chuckled. "Neither did I. As you know, I fully intended to be a nun. But I'm so grateful Sir Robert entered my life. He enhances every part of it."

"Your love for each other is obvious. But have you ever…wanted more?"

Constance's brow furrowed, then smoothed. "What more could I want? Druid's Head is a lovely home, and I enjoy my duties there. The people have welcomed me as one of their own. I also have my charity work with Father Leof in Preostbi." A faraway look and secretive smile overtook her features. "And every day, as dusk falls, the anticipation starts."

Ardyth glanced into the shop. The tailor crouched over his sewing, while at a nearby table, his apprentice cut red cloth with large, cross-bladed scissors. "Anticipation? Of what, pray?"

"Of what the night will bring…with Robert." Constance's voice was soft, yearning.

Ardyth's gaze shot back to her. *Whoa! If she forgot to say "sir," he must be some lover!*

The lady's cheeks had turned pink. "My husband is…extraordinary. So are his brothers, in their own ways. May I offer a word of advice?"

"You may."

"Your self-reliance is admirable, and from what I've heard, your scriptwork is inspired. But leave the door open to love. When two people share that depth of feeling, the rewards are…"

"What?"

Constance folded her hands together, as if intending to pray, then arched an eyebrow. "That's what I hope *you'll* discover."

****

After a successful hunt, Hugh and Robert rode side by side toward home. Seacrest, in all its glory, rose before them, still some distance away. Behind them trailed Isobel and Juliana, followed by the huntsman, assistant huntsmen, horn blowers, beaters, archers, dog handlers, and hounds.

Hugh breathed deeply of the fresh air and sighed with satisfaction. "I'm glad we had this last hunt together."

Robert smiled. "I am too. Hard to believe we're leaving on the morrow."

"You're welcome to stay. Mother would love it."

"We cannot. I promised to be at William's side for the birth of his child, and Lady Ravenwood is nearing her time."

"Will Lady Constance also stay at Ravenwood?"

Robert shook his head. "For a day or two, then I'll escort her to Druid's Head and hurry back. William shan't rest easy until his wife and the babe come safely through the ordeal."

"Surely the curse, if there ever was one, is broken."

"The child was conceived in love, so it must be." He cleared his throat. "Speaking of love…"

God's teeth! Hither it comes! "Let's not."

"Why ever not?"

He cast a wary glance at his brother. Knowing Robert, he'd find a way to speak his mind; if not now, sometime before he left…possibly in front of others.

"Say it, then."

"We've spent most of the day with Isobel, and I detected a certain…distance between the two of you."

"Distance?"

"Not on her part, but yours. You could've been more attentive."

Hugh shrugged. "I could've been less attentive, as well."

"True, but I wondered…" Robert's shoulders lifted as he took a deep breath. "You've known Lady Ardyth for more than a fortnight now. What do you think of her?"

"I'm trying *not* to think of her."

"Why?"

He huffed. "She has many…"

"Talents?"

"Oddities."

Robert chortled. "Such as?"

"She swims as well any man."

"Does she?"

Hugh nodded. "When she's warm, she twists her braid up onto her head and holds it thus, while fanning her neck with the other hand."

"Odd but understandable. Go on."

"You've heard her sing in that strange tongue which sounds Saxon and Norman and yet…neither. One day I came upon her alone in the solar. Her back was to me, so she didn't know I was there. She was singing a most peculiar, rhythmic song and moving her hips in a dance that was…"

"What, Brother?"

"Most provocative." His manhood stiffened, and he shifted in his saddle.

Robert cocked an eyebrow. "Really?"

"Another day, when no one was around, she lifted her skirts up to her thighs and ran on the beach."

"If no one was around, how did *you* see it?"

Hugh gave him a meaningful look.

Robert grinned. "The secret passage?"

"Aye. I intended to surprise her, but then…"

"What, in God's name?"

"I'm sure you've seen acrobats do that sideways turn…when they go upside down to stand on their hands, then land on one foot at a time. Well, she did something similar but landed with both feet together. Then she jumped in the air and flipped backward, landing perfectly on the sand. I've never seen anything like it."

Robert's gray eyes widened. "Extraordinary. And did you surprise her?"

"No. My shock stopped me. She's unlike any woman I've ever known. Where did she learn such things?"

"Lady Constance can juggle. A jester taught her. Perhaps an acrobat taught Lady Ardyth."

"But the swimming…the strange songs…the dance…acts of immodesty which other noblewomen wouldn't even consider…"

Robert's dimples appeared. "All of which have seized your attention in a way I've never beheld. Hugh, she's unique, just as you and your ideals have always been. And you must admit, her stories are wonderful."

"Indeed. Even Father Jacques attends them. Have you noticed that Giles has written several new songs? More than usual."

"No doubt he's trying to compete. And yet another

song about the treasure."

Hugh frowned. "I'm not sure I like him expanding on the legend."

"What harm could it do?"

"I don't know exactly, but it makes me uneasy."

"And while Giles competes, Ranulf stands in awe of the lady's gifts."

"Stands?" Hugh's chest tightened. "He might as well kneel at her feet. He fawns and simpers and makes a general nuisance of himself. Daily."

"I haven't noticed the lady objecting to his attentions."

"Hmph."

Robert's dimples grew deeper every moment. "The thought of them together grieves you."

"Hmph."

"As ever, your eloquence astounds me."

Hugh released a harsh sigh. "Fine. I admit it. It grieves me."

"Then do something about it."

Hugh's heart beat faster, but he willed it to calm. The lady was his scribe, and she showed no interest in any part of him, except his family history. While other women, including Isobel, clamored for his favor, Ardyth all but ran away. "I'm not sure I want to."

"Well, you'd better decide fast." Robert sobered and gave him a soulful look. "Lady Ardyth won't be here forever."

Chapter Seven

The next morning, after Robert, Constance, Guy, and Alice had departed, Ardyth invited Lillian to join her in the solar before Hugh arrived to inspect her work. Lady Seacrest raised an eyebrow, but after a brief deliberation, she assented. The spacious room was hot, even with the open windows.

Pining for air conditioning, Ardyth wiped sweat from her brow. *It's gonna be a scorcher!* She turned to Lillian. "Your ladyship is most kind to honor my request."

Lady Seacrest gave her a nod and motioned to one of the cushioned, high-backed chairs before the idle fireplace. "Prithee, sit."

Once they were both seated, Ardyth folded her hands in her lap. "I'm enjoying recording the family history."

The lady gave her another nod. "Lord Seacrest and I are quite pleased with your scriptwork and illumination."

"I'm glad, and grateful to be of service." She sat forward in her chair. "Soon Hugh shall tell me of his father, but I wondered if you would too."

"I?"

"I want to learn all I can…for the record…and I would guess you knew him better than most."

"That is true."

"Have you any objections?"

Lillian hesitated, then shook her head. "I haven't. You might also speak with Ranulf. His father, Lord Harcourt, and my husband were friends."

Ardyth smiled. Ranulf was friendly and candid. He was sure to know at least one interesting tidbit. "Thank you for the suggestion. I'll talk to him anon. So…Hugh said his father's given name was Simon. Pray, tell me about him."

A wistful expression swept over Lillian's features, and she instantly appeared younger. "Simon was…unlike any man I'd ever met. He visited my father in France, and from the moment I first saw him, I knew…" She fell silent. Emotion swam in her gray eyes.

Out of respect, Ardyth waited for her to continue. The silence stretched five seconds, then ten. She cleared her throat. "Forgive me, your ladyship. What did you know?"

Lillian blinked, then looked her straight in the eye. "That he would be mine. I trow he found me attractive but knew not the depth of my feelings. When he sailed for England the next day, 'twas as if a part of me had gone with him. Shortly thereafter, my father sent him a ship full of goods, and I stole aboard it."

Ardyth raised her eyebrows. "In secret?"

"Aye. I hid myself well, and by the time the crew discovered me, we'd gone too far to turn back."

"How old were you?"

"Eighteen. I was headstrong and unwilling to let anything, even the tempestuous sea, separate me from my desire."

"Eighteen?" Ardyth frowned. As a noblewoman,

Lillian should've been betrothed by then. "Weren't you betrothed to anyone?"

She nodded. "Ever since childhood. But a betrothal, like any other contract, can be broken. My father handled it with dignity. Of course, I gave him little choice in the matter, and his anger quelled once he learned 'twas Simon who rescued me."

"Rescued you?"

"From the shipwreck."

Ardyth's jaw dropped. "*The* shipwreck? The one that inspired Giles's songs?"

"The very same. My bold behavior shocked Simon, but soon after, he confessed his love for me." She motioned to one corner of the room, where a wooden screen emblazoned with a unicorn stood eight feet high. "That was one of his wedding presents to me. He knew unicorns fascinated me."

"'Tis beautiful."

"Our marriage was a happy one. He had a high regard for my opinion, and we made many plans together." Her face fell. "The one thing we didn't plan was his death."

Ardyth's heart twisted. She wanted to hug the woman, or at least give her a gentle pat of reassurance. But would either move offend her? Maybe. She kept her hands in her lap. "Was he at all like your sons?"

"You've only to look at Lord Seacrest to see my husband."

No wonder she fell for him! "But his lordship has your eyes."

Lady Seacrest arched an eyebrow. "You've noticed his eyes, have you? Aye, they are mine. The rest of him is all Simon, including his temperament."

Ardyth's stomach tightened. "His temperament. Can you describe it?"

"Passionate. Loyal. Determined to do things his way." Lillian's gaze slipped toward the fireplace. "Simon died before he could arrange for our son's betrothal, and while I should've assumed that duty, I didn't. You see, I understand Hugh's wishes, as odd as they appear to others. Should I subject him to less felicity in marriage than I myself enjoyed?"

"No. I agree with you, and with him. He deserves to be happy."

Lillian met her gaze, and a slow smile spread across her face. "He does, and like his father, he shall be fiercely devoted to the mate he chooses. She'll be a fortunate woman indeed."

And she won't be me. It'll be Isobel. Or Juliana. Or someone else he's yet to meet. A sudden weight tugged at Ardyth's heart. *If only...no! Ridiculous! I know where I belong, and that's that.*

****

Hugh spotted Giles standing in front of the castle well, chatting with the alewife. He strode toward them, past the brewery, and the malty smell of fresh ale filled his nostrils.

The alewife saw him first and dropped a curtsy. "My lord."

Giles, who'd been peering into the deep, stone-lined shaft, straightened, and his head whipped toward Hugh. "My lord. How may I serve?"

"I would speak with you. Alone."

The alewife scuttled toward the brewery, and Giles matched Hugh step for step as they walked from the well toward the keep.

Hugh glanced at the minstrel. "The legend of the Seacrest treasure figures largely in your new songs. Why?"

Giles cleared his throat. "It has always intrigued the people."

"Granted. But what of the ghost lights floating along the cliffside? There's no need to embellish the tale with more lies."

"My lord, I sang true. Many seamen have reported seeing the lights after dark. Just ask Philippe. He's also heard them talk of it."

Hugh rubbed his jaw. The gatekeeper was an honest man. So was Giles. If they'd both heard such reports, could there be truth to them?

"I see. I thought you invented it."

"Why? To contend with Ranulf's songs? Or Lady Ardyth's stories?"

"The thought occurred to me. By the way, what is your opinion of Lady Ardyth's tales?"

Giles hesitated. "Her imagination is notable."

"But?"

A grumble sounded low in the minstrel's throat. "May I speak freely?"

"You may."

"I'm troubled, my lord. Do you trust her?"

Hugh looked sharply at him. "Why do you ask?"

Giles shrugged. "'Tis only a feeling. There's something…different about her."

More than something, Hugh thought. But was it cause for distrust?

He dismissed Giles and hurried into the keep. Lady Ardyth would be waiting for him in the solar, and he had a surprise for her. With any luck, 'twould be a welcome one.

As he neared the arched entrance, her voice caressed his ears. "Very fortunate."

Hugh frowned. She sounded sad.

"Is aught amiss?" His mother's voice. What was she doing here?

"No," Ardyth replied. "Naught."

He strolled into the chamber. "Am I interrupting?"

Both women started, then stood and turned to him as one. If he didn't know better, he'd think they looked…guilty.

His mother smiled. "Not at all. But now you've come, I'll leave you to your work. Lady Ardyth." She nodded, first at the younger woman and then at him. "Son." Without another word, she glided out of the room.

Ardyth stepped forward. Her rose-colored gown brought out the color in her cheeks. "We were discussing your father."

"Oh?"

She nodded, then wiped away the sweat that glistened between her nose and upper lip. Those lips. Plump and pink. The gateway through which her voice blessed all around her.

He caught himself before his thoughts could gain speed. *Enough!* Had she bewitched him? Never had a woman inspired such musings in him.

She wiped her brow. "I wanted to hear your mother's impressions of him."

"Did you fear you wouldn't be able to trust mine?"

"Not at all! I simply wanted another opinion, and from what you've told me, she knew him well."

"That she did."

She gave him a closed-mouth smile. "So…are you ready to review my work?"

Indecision gripped him, but only for an instant. He took a deep breath. "In a moment. First, I want to give you something." He crossed to the semicircular oak table along the wall and grabbed the quill pen he'd fashioned the night before. Then he moved to stand an arm's length away from her. "Here." He handed her the plume.

She took it from him and studied it in silence. At last, she looked up. "Where did you get this?"

"From an obliging barn owl."

Her brown eyes widened. "Do you mean to say…you made it?"

"I did." Clearing his throat, he clasped his hands behind his back. "For you."

Her gaze dropped to the feather. Again, she examined it…for longer than he would've liked. What was she thinking? Had he overstepped his bounds?

"If you felt I needed a new pen, then…has my script displeased you in some way?"

"No." He swallowed hard. "Your father called you his 'little owl,' so I thought…" The sentence trailed off to nowhere. *This was a mistake. 'Twas folly to think…*

"Thank you." She met his gaze. Unshed tears shimmered in her eyes. "I cannot believe you remembered that. And I…I didn't realize how much I missed my father…and my mother…until this moment."

His relief leapt aside as a surge of compassion flooded through him. "Do they live?"

"Oh, aye."

"Perhaps they could visit you here."

She averted her gaze. "No. They're too far away."

"Too far? Does infirmity prevent them from traveling?"

She hesitated. "Something like that." She blinked rapidly and shook her head as if to clear it. Then she lifted both her gaze and the owl feather. "'Tis a wonderful gift."

Her sincerity shone in her eyes and chimed in her voice. She smiled, and his heart skipped a beat. He hadn't blundered after all. He'd made her happy, and that made *him* happier than he'd been in quite a while.

"I'm glad you like it."

"I love it, Hugh."

His eyes widened at the intimacy. "You used my given name."

Her wide eyes mirrored his. "I did! Forgive me, my lord."

"No, I like the way it sounded. You may continue to use it, if you prefer."

"I do prefer it." She grinned. "May I ask that you call me by *my* given name?"

He returned her smile. "You may, and I shall…Ardyth."

She stared into his eyes for a long moment, then turned abruptly and started toward the writing desk. "Come and see what I finished yesterday while you were hunting."

She settled onto the stool and stuck her new pen next to the old one in the desk's secondary holder, beside the hole that housed the ink pot. Then she twisted up her braid and fanned her nape.

In four long strides, he stood at her back. Close enough to bend down and kiss her glistening neck…which was all he wanted to do at the moment.

No! The gift went well enough, but I mustn't rush things. Slowly now.

She stopped fanning herself and pointed to the parchment. "This section here."

As he leaned over to get a closer look, he forgot the manuscript and found himself staring at a rogue, damp tendril of blonde hair curled behind her ear. The mingled scents of the sea and her sweat filled his senses. Salty and sweet. Alluring.

She'd gone swimming again. In her chemise, which had surely clung to her every curve, as it did that first day he accompanied her. His manhood stirred at the memory. He wanted to wrap his arms around her, lift her off the stool, and leave a trail of kisses all the way down her back to the…

Control yourself! But her nearness called to every inch of his body, and he grew harder by the second. Her name hovered in his mind, as lovely and lilting as the songs she sang each night. *Ardyth.*

Chapter Eight

Hugh's breath was hot on her neck. His body heat insinuated itself into her back. The solar was hot enough without him adding steam to the sauna. Yet her flesh tingled. He was at once too close and not close enough. She had half a mind to whirl around, grab him by the tunic, and plant a kiss on his lips that would shock the hell out of him.

What he might do then...

What she might do...

She was wet between the legs, and not just with sweat. *Argh! Underwear would be good right about now!* But there was none. There was only her chemise and gown and a hot medieval man breathing down her neck. Literally! She felt strangely exposed, yet excited.

Ardyth.

She gasped, then recovered herself. "Hugh?"

"What?" His voice was low, husky. What emotion would his face betray?

She couldn't look; it was best not to know. She kept her gaze glued to the parchment. "Did you just say my name?"

There was a pause. A long one. "No."

"That's odd. I could swear..." She broke off as another sound—a rustling just outside the solar—reached her ears.

She sprang to her feet and brushed past Hugh,

intent on reaching the archway. Once there, she glanced outside.

The space was empty.

She frowned. "I know I heard something."

It was the third time that week someone had skulked outside the solar while she and Hugh were working. She'd ignored it before, but this time, she'd hoped to catch the eavesdropper in the act.

Was Isobel spying on them? Was Juliana? Or was someone else listening?

Hugh was watching her. His gray eyes were intense as a stormy sky.

"What?" she asked. "Why do you look at me that way?"

He looked toward the open shutters. "No reason."

Frowning further, she followed his gaze to the window. Then she smiled and snapped her fingers. "I have an idea."

He gave her a wary look. "Which is?"

"The day is too hot and sticky to stay indoors. Shall we go outside? Mayhap down to the shore?"

"You would write there?"

"No, but I could listen to you. I've a good memory, and I can write out everything later."

He stroked his chin. "I don't know…"

"We could swim. Both of us."

His hand dropped from his jaw. "The idea does have a certain appeal."

"Of course it does. This solar is hotter than sin."

He crossed the short distance between them and gave her a lopsided grin that made her stomach quiver. "That hot, is it?"

She licked her lips. "Aye. What say you?"

He hesitated. "'Tis almost time for the midday meal. We're expected."

"Perhaps we can forego that and just this once, eat by ourselves."

He quirked his eyebrows, and lines creased his forehead. "You're serious."

"Never more so, and I'm taking charge."

He gave her a wry smile. "You do realize this is my solar, my keep, my land…"

"Your everything, I know. But let me see to the food."

"Ardyth."

"Hugh."

Their stare-off lasted a good ten seconds. Then he chuckled. "Very well. Shall we meet at the postern gate?"

"Aye, but give me a little time. I'll be there anon." She spun around and struck off for the kitchens.

If the solar was a sauna, the kitchens were hell on earth. However, the tempting smells of roasting meat and bubbling stew almost made up for it. The bulky and balding head cook, Aubert, stood at one of a long table, instructing a teenaged undercook who pounded meat into a paste.

He looked up as she approached the table. "Ah, Lady Ardyth. Come again to watch our preparations?"

"Actually, I've come to make my own."

He gave her a quizzical look. "Your own?"

She nodded. "A simple meal for two, for Lord Seacrest and me. With the midday meal so close, I know you're busy, so I'll make the food myself."

He and the undercook shared a long look. "I doubt his lordship would approve."

"His lordship knows I'm here."

"He knows what you're about?"

She shifted her feet. "Mostly."

Cook and undercook shared a second, longer glance.

Her hands found her hips. "Aubert, I intend to do this."

With a sigh, he regarded her. "Allow me to help, my lady. What do you have in mind?"

Success! "Have you any spit-roasted beef?"

"I have."

"How did you baste it?"

"With red wine, vinegar, salt, pepper, and ginger."

She beamed at him. "That sounds perfect. I'll need four slices of bread, two slices of the beef, and two slices of Cheshire cheese, all of similar size. And…" She turned to an adjacent table, atop which sat a variety of fresh vegetables, and pointed. "A little of that lettuce."

"Shall I boil it? We also have pickled lettuce."

"No, I'd like it fresh."

His eyes bulged. "Fresh?"

"Aye. And I'll need a flask of ale and cloth in which to wrap the food."

"At once, my lady."

He called orders to three undercooks and tore the lettuce himself. Within minutes, everything she'd requested lay on the table before her. She prepared two sandwiches, then wrapped them in the cloth. Curious eyes watched her all the while. Little Corbin and his mother, Millicent, were among the onlookers, and when asked if she would sing and tell a story again that night, Ardyth assured them she would.

She smiled at Aubert in parting. "Thank you for your help."

He scratched his head, his gaze still riveted to the packed food. "Of course, my lady."

With the flask and food in hand, she scurried outside to the upper bailey. Hugh stood before the postern gate, talking with gatekeeper.

She navigated the garden with brisk steps and halted in front of them. "Good day, Philippe."

The gatekeeper gave her a nod. "Good day, my lady." As usual, he sounded as if someone had attacked his vocal cords with sandpaper.

She regarded Hugh. "Shall we?"

"In all haste. Allow me." He grabbed the flask and food bundle, which he promptly sniffed. "It smells good. What's inside?"

She gave him an enigmatic smile. "You'll see."

They started down the path to the beach. The breeze off the ocean was heaven, and the cries of seagulls and splashing of waves soothed her soul. Seacrest and its lord were equally beautiful, and Hugh had given her the most thoughtful gift imaginable. Unique to her talents and experience. The compassion that glowed in his eyes when she mentioned her parents had taken her breath away.

John had never looked at her that way. Nor had he taken the time to make her a present. She had to admit the attention was nice.

"You're deep in thought," Hugh remarked. "About what?"

She shrugged off her memories. "Nothing important. Pray, tell me of your father."

He had nothing but praise for the former Lord

Seacrest. He talked at length as they followed the shore around the rugged headland and as they sat side by side on the sand, shaded by the roof of the sea cave. She basked in the sound of his deep voice and the view of the crashing waves before them.

After a while, she unpacked the food and handed him his portion. Her mouth watered in anticipation.

He lifted the top slice of bread with interest. "What is this?"

"I call it a 'sandwich.'"

"Sand-wich?" he pronounced slowly. "A Saxon word?"

"Aye."

He frowned at his share. "The lettuce is uncooked."

"Naturally."

"Naturally?"

"Trust me and take a bite."

He gave her a dubious look, then did as she asked. His eyes widened as he chewed.

She smiled. "Good?"

He swallowed. "Delicious."

She bit into her sandwich and relished the combination of flavors and textures. *You're no Philly cheesesteak, but you're close enough!*

They ate in quiet companionship, sipping the ale in turns and staring out at the sibilant sea. When they finished, he turned to her.

"Thank you for that."

She folded the cloth neatly. "Thank *you* for the owl pen. So…are you ready to swim?"

"I am." With a grin, he reached for his boots and proceeded to remove them and his hose.

She followed suit, then stood. Hugh's gaze locked

onto her bare ankles.

"Hugh," she said, loud enough to carry over the ocean's song.

He blinked, then looked up at her. "Aye?"

"Aren't you going to doff the rest of your clothing?"

"Oh, aye." Standing, he wiped the crumbs from his tunic and removed it while she doffed her own. Then he pulled his undertunic over his head, leaving him clad in only his calf-length, linen breeches.

Her gaze shot to his torso and stayed there. His muscles were well-defined beneath the black hair that covered them. Strong, but without the bodybuilder bulges that had always turned her off. His physique was…in a word, perfect.

"My lady?"

She swallowed hard and lifted her stare to his face, which seemed just as perfect. The wind caught her chemise, tickling her flesh like a lover. She scarcely remembered what that was like; it felt like forever since she'd slept with a man.

Hugh's smile melted away, and his eyes darkened. He advanced toward her and halted a foot away. "Ardyth."

His voice. His nearness. His *essence*. All overwhelmed her.

She could hardly breathe but found the will to speak. "Let's swim." With a herculean effort, she turned and ran toward the surf.

In a flash, he was beside her, and they waded into the ocean. The bracing water erased the summer heat in an instant.

When they were waist deep, she beamed at Hugh.

"Isn't this better than working indoors?"

He returned her smile. "Infinitely better." He watched the waves in silence for a few seconds, then turned back to her. "That first day we came to the sea...at the end of your swim, a wave carried you toward shore."

She searched her memory. *Right. I was bodysurfing.* "I remember."

"Did you plan for that to happen, or was it a matter of chance?"

"I planned it."

"From whom did you learn the skill?"

A college roommate from Florida, who invited me home with her three spring breaks in a row. "A friend," she said aloud.

He frowned. "A man?"

She shook her head. "A woman."

"But how did she…"

"Her father taught her." It was the only response he might believe. "Shall I teach *you* how to do it?"

He nodded in answer.

"Fine. It works best if you make your body an arrow, with your hands above your head, but you have to wait for the right moment. Watch, and I'll show you."

Before long, he was bodysurfing like a pro. Yes, his gaze strayed to her wet chemise—that is, the breasts within it—several times, but that was to be expected. Twice, she herself caught a glimpse of the dark hair and bulge visible through his breeches, but she forced herself to focus on the task at hand.

The warmth of the sun, the cresting waves, and the sheer fun of swimming with Hugh brought laughter to her lips. She turned to him. "This is wonderful, isn't it?"

Undiluted pleasure sparkled in his eyes. "Aye. I haven't swum in years."

"Well, I'm glad I suggested it."

"As am I."

The water grew more demanding, pulling hard on her legs, for there was a strong undertow. She glanced up at the clifftop castle to gage the distance they'd drifted. "The current is getting stronger. Perhaps we should go back to the cave."

He followed her gaze to Seacrest and nodded. "A good idea."

They moved toward shore. When the water was thigh deep, a powerful wave pushed her off balance, and she fell toward Hugh. Just in time, he caught her, grasping her upper arms and pulling her back upright.

Hyper-aware of his body pressed to hers, she looked up into his eyes. His gaze burned hotter than the sun.

****

Hugh stared into the depths of her gold-flecked, brown eyes. He tightened his grip on her arms, then forced himself to relax it. His voice seemed lodged in his throat, unable to break free.

What would she do if I kissed her? He lowered his head toward her. *Just...like...*

"Thank you." Regaining her footing, she pulled away and hurried toward shore.

God's blood! She was running away from him. Again. Had he imagined the desire in her eyes? No. Not only had he seen it; he'd felt it, reaching out to him on a level she might not acknowledge. But *he* recognized it.

First in the cave when he'd disrobed, and now here, where the land met the sea.

He rubbed his mouth and strode after her. Her wet chemise clung to the ample curves of her backside as she hastened back to the cave. Oh, but she was luscious!

Yet again, his manhood stirred. *No! Control!* 'Twouldn't do for her to have visible proof of his own desire.

He entered the dark, cool hollow and went to stand beside her. She'd stopped roughly ten yards from the back of the cave and stared at the tunnel openings on the ledge above.

Time to make conversation. He cleared his throat. "My brothers and I used to play here as boys. The tunnels provided excellent hiding places and sparked our imaginations."

With a self-conscious smile, she pulled her wet chemise away from her body and turned to him. "I've yet to meet Lord Ravenwood, but I can certainly imagine you and Sir Robert scampering about as boys. What fun you must've had!"

He grinned at a particular memory of William and Robert hunting for him as he hid inside one of the tunnels. They had such a difficult time finding him, they believed he'd vanished altogether. When at last he reappeared, he gave them a mysterious look and said, "Who knows? Perhaps these tunnels are steeped in magic, and for a brief moment, I entered another world."

Ardyth studied his face. "'Tis obvious you have fond memories of childhood. The three of you were close?"

"We were. And then…"

"What?"

"William went to live in another household to begin his path toward knighthood. Soon afterward, Robert joined him there. They stayed close, their destinies entwined." Suddenly, speech felt laborious, and silence took hold.

"While you were left behind to take on the baron's mantle, responsible for all of Seacrest." She bit her lip. "I was an only child, so I know something of loneliness. You must've missed your brothers terribly and wondered what adventures they enjoyed while you stayed home." Sympathy darkened her eyes.

He nodded and found his tongue. "How well you put it." No one, not even his mother, had understood his discontent at the time. Yet here was this bewitching Saxon scribe, giving a voice to his inner thoughts as though they were her own.

All at once, her hand rested on his upper arm. 'Twas still cold from the sea, but soft. Her eyes were soft as well. Lovely and beguiling. "I'm sorry, Hugh."

He swallowed hard. "Sorry?"

"That you were left behind…and lonely."

Her compassion warmed his heart, and his body. Perhaps some of that warmth infused her hand, for it had lost its chill. "Thank you, Ardyth." His voice sounded far away.

Her hand fell away from his arm. She blinked and took a step backward. "Forgive me. I shouldn't have touched you."

"I don't mind."

She held his gaze for a long moment, then gasped. "I forgot to bring a dry chemise. I was so intent on preparing our food, it consumed my thoughts."

Awareness dawned, and he grinned. "And I forgot to grab an extra pair of breeches."

"You did?" She tilted her head to the side. "You cannot use food as your excuse. What were *you* thinking of?"

He hesitated, but honesty was the best course. "I believe I thought only of you."

Again, she stared into his eyes. Then she glanced toward their clothing, piled tidily on the sand, and pulled her wet chemise away from her tantalizing flesh. "I'll drench my clothes if I put them on over this. Because of the cut of the gown, I cannot do without a smock. I suppose I must wait here until the one I'm wearing dries."

"Or..." Should he tell her? Could she be trusted? He looked into her wide brown eyes and divined she could. "There's another way up to the keep. A secret passage, so no one will see us. Grab your things, and I'll show you."

He, too, seized his clothes, as well as the food cloth and flask, and headed for the roughly hewn steps on the rock wall to the right. She followed him up the steps to the ledge, then along it to the right, all the way to the mouth of the cave and around to the short, narrow path on the cliffside. At the "Rock Man"—so dubbed by William when he was but six years old and in awe of the seven-foot-high rock jutting out from the cliff—he paused and turned to Ardyth.

"How are you with enclosed spaces?"

She shrugged. "All right, I guess."

"Good. Follow me."

He rounded the left side of the Rock Man, where

the path led into the tunnel. He went a short distance, then paused beside the thin opening on their right. He pointed to the gap. "There's a small ledge there, if you need a breath of fresh air."

She shook her head. "I assure you, I'm fine. Lead on."

"Very well. Give me your clothes."

"Why?"

"'Tis dark inside, and you'll need to mind your footing. Hold onto my waist and stay close."

She handed him the clothing. When he turned to continue on, her small, warm hands pressed gently into his sides. Her touch on his bare flesh, and the heat of her breath on his back, set his heart racing.

"I'm ready," she pronounced. "Onward."

With a grin, he entered the darkness. The cool, dank tunnel went straight for a little way before veering to the left. He walked slowly for her sake…and for his own, to savor and prolong the feel of her behind him. At last, they reached the steps. "Now we climb. Hold tight."

Up, up they climbed, until the fingers of his free hand brushed the textured, raised grain of the oaken trapdoor above his head. "Quiet now while I open the trapdoor, in case anyone is around." With care, he pushed the door upward, and light spilled over and around them. Twelve stairs more, and he stepped onto the wooden floor. He listened for any sound and peeked around the corner of the eight-foot-high wooden screen.

They were alone. Turning, he reached out a hand to help Ardyth up.

She gave his hand a long look, then took it and completed the climb. With furrowed brow, she glanced at the stone wall behind them and the screen in front. "Where are we?"

Reluctantly, he released her hand and closed the trapdoor. "The solar."

She nodded slowly and pointed. "So this is the back of the unicorn screen."

"Aye."

"It definitely hides the trapdoor."

"And anyone entering or exiting it. Come."

"Whither?"

He hesitated only an instant. "To my bedchamber."

She raised her eyebrows in silent surprise.

He sighed. "You'll be quite safe from my attentions, I assure you. Make haste."

They crept from behind the screen, crossed the solar, and hurried to the stairwell. He led her up the spiral steps to the chamber door, which stood ajar, then motioned for her to enter before him.

She walked a few steps into the room and paused, scanning the interior he knew so well. The geometric shapes painted on the limewashed walls. The tapestries, oak furnishings, massive fireplace, and deep red curtains encasing the bed.

"So this is where you sleep." Her drenched chemise clung to her right calf, giving him a lovely view of the fair, tapered flesh of her ankle.

He held his position in the doorway. "Aye."

"It looks a lot more comfortable than my mattress."

If you'd care to join me, I'd see to your comfort…in every way. His heart beat faster, and for an instant, he feared he'd spoken aloud.

She turned to him and gave him a sheepish grin. "I don't mean to criticize your hospitality. I'm grateful for what comfort I *do* have."

"I understand."

Her chest rose and fell with a deep breath. Her nipples pointed plainly beneath the wet smock. "What now?"

Now I take you in my arms, lead you to the bed, and show you there are some things only a man *can do.* He was rigid and ready; thankfully, the clothing he carried hid that fact.

As if sensing his arousal, she took a step backward, inadvertently moving closer to the bed. 'Twould be so easy to…

No! The time wasn't right. He'd told her she'd be safe from his attentions, and he would keep his word. "Now I don dry clothes." He stepped over the threshold.

"What about me?"

"Once I'm dressed, I'll go and get one of your chemises."

"*You'll* get it?"

"Unless you want the servants to gossip."

"I see your point." Her gaze dropped to the wad of clothes in his hands.

He flashed her a droll grin. "You'll see more than that unless you look away this moment."

"Oh?" Her eyes widened with understanding. "Oh." She turned away and focused on the stag tapestry beside the fireplace.

With a sigh, he dropped his bundle on the table. He crossed to one of his chests, grabbed a dry pair of breeches, and changed quickly.

Before long, he pulled on his second boot and stood. "You may look now. I shall retrieve your chemise. Have you more than one trunk?"

"Aye. Two, next to the smaller mattress. I keep my smocks folded in the front left corner of the larger one."

"Right."

"Um…Hugh."

"Aye?"

"What if Lady Isobel or Lady Juliana is there?"

He shrugged. "With any luck, neither will be."

Luck was not his friend. The instant he stepped into the guest chamber, Isobel whirled to face him with wide eyes, and a moment later, flushed cheeks.

"My lord, what brings you hither?"

God's nails! He averted his gaze and looked from the large mattress to the smaller one. Two chests stood beside it; the bigger one was open. He pointed. "Are those Lady Ardyth's trunks?"

"Aye. Why do you ask?"

"She has need of something."

"Something?"

He brushed past her and bent over the open trunk. The pile of smocks was just where Ardyth said, at the front left corner. He seized the top one, then hesitated. The garment was so light and soft. 'Twas odd to think that what veiled her lovely body now rested in his hand.

"Her *chemise*?" Isobel nearly choked on the word.

He rolled his eyes and turned to face her. "The one she's wearing is wet…from swimming."

She glanced at his slick hair. "Did *you* swim as well?" There was an edge to her voice.

He frowned. "I did. Have you a problem with that?"

Her blue eyes flared before she looked away. "No, my lord. But…" Her gaze challenged his once again.

"Why did it fall on you to fetch her chemise? Are you her servant?"

Heat raced through him, and a muscle twitched in his jaw. The chamber grew more cramped every moment. "Jealousy does not become you."

She pouted. "I am not jealous. I am...fie!" She let out a huff, then composed herself. "Where is she now?"

He'd be damned if he'd disclose that information. Clutching the chemise in his hand, he started toward the archway. "Waiting for me."

Chapter Nine

"...and they lived in happiness forevermore." Ardyth fell silent, and after a pregnant pause, the great hall erupted with applause.

She smiled at little Corbin, who clapped wildly; beside him, Millicent wiped joyful tears from her eyes. Grateful her story had touched them, Ardyth lifted her gaze to the gallery, where Lady Seacrest and Hugh nodded their approval. The lady granted a grin, but her son wore a pensive expression.

What was he thinking? And what happened when he went to get her smock? Earlier, when he returned to his chamber, he threw the garment her way, told her to dress, and announced he had important matters to which he must attend. He had his duties, of course. He *was* Lord Seacrest, and when he wasn't holding court, inspecting his lands, or checking the progress of her work, he often met with Bertram, the steward, to ensure the smooth running of the estate. But his brusque departure smacked of something more. What, she couldn't guess.

"Another triumph, my lady." All smiles, Ranulf stepped in front of her. Conversation and movement filled the hall behind him.

"Thank you." She stood, stepped to the side of the high stool she'd just vacated, and motioned toward it. "Pray, sit. I want to ask you a question."

Ranulf quirked an eyebrow but did as she asked, cradling his knees with his hands. "Ask what you will."

"What do you know of the former Lord Seacrest? Lady Seacrest tells me he and your father were friends."

He nodded. "Fast friends. He was an honorable man and a fair one. Clever, too. And…" Fingering the cleft in his chin, he leaned closer. "I wouldn't divulge this to just anyone, but I shall tell *you*. Years ago, not long after the famed shipwreck, Simon confided in my father. He said fate awarded him riches of which few could boast."

"Treasure?"

He shrugged. "'Twould seem a foolish notion, I know. Yet my father believed in the treasure right up until his death. Tell me, has Lord Seacrest ever mentioned…" His gaze shifted to something beyond her, and his brow furrowed.

She looked over her shoulder. Giles stood close behind her. Too close, for although his back was turned, he stood statue-still, with neither companion nor purpose, unless…

Was he listening to their conversation?

She spun around to face him. "Did you want something, Giles?"

He jumped, then turned to her. His gaze met hers only an instant before he averted it. "No, my lady. I…"

"Giles!" Isobel's voice carried over the cacophony of sounds in the hall. She made a summoning gesture with one hand. Beside her, Juliana watched quietly, biting her lip.

The minstrel looked from Ardyth to Isobel and back again. "I am wanted." He hurried off toward the sisters. The trio exchanged a few words, then turned as one to regard Ardyth and Ranulf.

Had Giles been spying for his own benefit or the ladies'?

Ardyth glanced up at Hugh, whose hands clasped the gallery railing as he stared down at her and the goliard. His brow was definitely in brooding mode.

She sighed inwardly. *I'm OD'ing on intrigue!*

"We seem to be the focus of much interest," Ranulf remarked genially.

Ignoring the onlookers, she gave him her full attention. "Apparently so. Why, I wonder?"

He gave her a conspiratorial grin. "We're two of a kind, you and I. I live a freer lifestyle than many of my station and criticize the Church in song. You're a female scribe who performs like a minstrel and bathes in the sea without care. We both rebel against custom, and that invites curiosity."

Yes, curiosity from every corner. "I suppose you're right." His smile was contagious. He really was handsome, and friendly as all get-out.

On impulse, she lifted her gaze to the gallery. Lord Seacrest and his mother were gone.

The next day, she felt Hugh's absence while writing in the solar. Memories from their impromptu beach picnic stole her focus again and again. His storm-gray eyes. His gorgeous body, strong and wet from the sea's embrace. The grip of his large hands on her upper arms when the wave had almost knocked her down. The heat of his torso beneath her hands and the salty smell of his flesh as he led her in the dark through the secret passage.

Her fingers tingled on the quill he'd made her, and she looked down at the instrument. So soft a feather.

Such a lovely, considerate gift. She'd never hold it again without recalling the expression on his face when he presented it; his desire to please her was unmistakable.

She managed to get a little work done but soon heeded the call of the sea breeze and shore. With a flask of elderberry wine and her replacement chemise in hand, she passed through the postern gate.

"Good day, Philippe."

"Good day, my lady," he rasped.

The wind was in rare form today, flailing her braid and molding her blue skirt to her legs as she trod down the path toward the beach. When she was halfway down, a familiar voice called from behind.

"Lady Ardyth! Wait!"

Ardyth turned to see Juliana skittering down the hill toward her. Exiting the gatehouse, Isobel shot Philippe a look of annoyance and hastened to catch up with her sister. Both women wore shades of yellow, made brighter by the hot summer sun.

"I hope you won't mind," Juliana said breathlessly. "I thought I'd join you this time and learn why you take such pleasure in these outings."

Isobel came alongside her. "And I thought I'd follow to make sure she does nothing foolish."

Ardyth carried on down the path. "There's nothing foolish about freedom."

Isobel raised an eyebrow. "Freedom?"

"Down on the beach, I'm free to be myself...to do anything I wish without worrying about another's judgment."

"We cannot escape judgment," Isobel said. "'Tis one of the few certainties in life."

Juliana nodded. "Especially for women."

Ardyth grimaced. *True enough, even in the twentieth century.*

Isobel cast a glance at the smock in Ardyth's hand. "I see you remembered your chemise. If only your memory had served you so well yesterday."

A tidal wave of comprehension swept over Ardyth: Hugh's mood swing the day before; his aloofness today. Isobel had caught him in the act of fetching the smock, and guilt reared its ugly head. *Then he dropped me like a hot potato!*

Clearly, he valued the medieval lady's opinion more than hers. Her heart sank, and she stared hard at the boats moored on the shore. As if in sympathy, ashen clouds fleeted across the sky, shielding her from the sun's glare as she and the sisters continued walking.

Juliana turned to Isobel. "What do you mean?"

Heat flooded through Ardyth. "She means to catch me off-guard and criticize my swim with Lord Seacrest yesterday."

Juliana's hands flew to her cheeks as they rounded the soaring cliff. "The two of you? Swimming together?"

"'Tis too true." Isobel glowered at the sand. "But you mistake my meaning, Lady Ardyth."

Like hell I do! Ardyth took a deep breath and slowly blew it out. "Let's not quarrel. The sun should return any moment now, and I could teach *you* to swim, if you like.

Isobel's eyes doubled in size. "Me?"

"Lady Juliana, too."

Juliana clinched her hands in front of her. "Would it be—"

"I can speak for us both," Isobel cut in. "The answer is no."

Juliana stopped short before the sea cave and scowled at her sister. It was the first show of defiance Ardyth had seen from her. "Isobel, if you're determined to be disagreeable, you can return to the keep. I wish to speak with Lady Ardyth."

Isobel's frown deepened. "About what, pray?"

"Does it matter?"

"It might. I'm perfectly willing to leave, but not before I know why you're *truly* here."

Juliana sighed. "I would speak of Ranulf."

Isobel gave her a knowing smile. "Ah, so that's what this is about. Very well. I'll leave you to it." Her gaze slid to Ardyth. "I trust no one will come looking for one of my sister's smocks."

Bite me, Isobel! "That depends entirely upon Juliana's wishes."

Isobel's grin dissolved. Curtly, she turned and marched back the way they came. The wind whipped her golden gown in a fury from behind, as if to speed her departure. A veritable ceiling of cloud veiled the sun above.

Juliana heaved another sigh. "Thank you for taking my part in that. My sister can be…overbearing at times."

"You're most welcome." *Maybe I could teach you how to do a roundoff back handspring. Then we'd really shock Isobel!* They continued walking, and she smiled as they entered the cave. "Perhaps 'tis better to have an overbearing sister than no sister at all."

"That's right; you have no siblings." Ten yards in, Juliana halted and surveyed the cave's cool, dim interior. "I haven't been down here in years. When Isobel and I were girls, Lord Seacrest and Sir Robert showed it to us. 'Tisn't as large as I remember, but I was quite small then."

Ardyth pulled the stopper from her flask and took a sip of wine. A mixture of tastes, tart and sweet, woke her taste buds. "May I offer you some elderberry wine?"

Juliana shook her head. "Thank you, no." Her brow creased, and she started to fidget. "So...about Ranulf..." She fell into a silence which lasted a good five seconds.

Ardyth stooped and placed her chemise and the wine on the sand. Then she straightened. "Go on."

"Last night, one of his songs was quite different from the rest. He sang of longing...for something one cannot have. You heard it?"

"I did."

"Well, I know that feeling, and I...oh, fie! You must tell me...have you designs on Ranulf?"

"Designs?" The poor girl practically trembled with suspense; she must be smitten with him. "Rest easy, Lady Juliana. I consider him a friend. That is all."

"In sooth?"

Ardyth nodded. "In fact, if the opportunity arises, I'll turn his attention toward you."

Juliana's eyes widened. Then she breathed a sigh of relief and flashed a smile as bright as the hidden sun. "God and His angels be praised! I was unsure whether...well, 'tis good of you to want to help me. I've admired him for such a long time."

"I can see why. Ranulf is smart, talented, and as far as I can tell, kind. 'Tis no hardship to look upon him, either!"

A male voice interjected. "Aye, with a chin chiseled by God Himself."

Hugh! There was a dangerous edge to his voice. She turned toward the mouth of the cave.

He stood with arms folded and feet well apart. A powerful figure whose fierce gaze matched the raging sea behind him. "Or so I hear."

Juliana strode toward him. "My lord, Lady Ardyth was just—"

"Singing the praises of Ranulf," he finished for her. "Pray, leave us, my lady."

She paused midstep. "But I would—"

"Lady Juliana…" His tone and expression brooked no refusal.

She lowered her gaze. "Aye, my lord. I'm leaving." With a nervous glance toward Ardyth, she scurried out of the cave and into the whistling wind beyond.

Ardyth crossed her arms, mirroring Hugh's stance. God, he was sexy! "You got your wish. We're alone. Now what?" She shivered. *On second thought, don't answer that.*

****

Hugh stormed into the cave, unable to stem the tide of jealousy swelling inside him. A pox on Ranulf! Ardyth thought him smart, talented, kind, and handsome. *She told* me *she didn't need a man. Now here she is, half in love with a goliard!*

Her arms dropped to her sides, and she stumbled backward.

He stopped and frowned. "Why do you recoil?"

She halted and lifted her chin. "Why do you look so angry?"

With purposeful strides, he closed the distance between them. "I met Lady Isobel near the gatehouse. She told me you were here, talking of Ranulf."

"Oh, she did! How good of her to report my every move, and how predictable that you prize her opinion above mine."

"As you prize Ranulf above other men?" He clenched his fists, willing her to contradict him yet knowing she wouldn't.

"What are you talking about?"

"I saw the pair of you last night…conversing cozily in the hall. 'Tis obvious he's claimed your affections, though how I cannot—"

"What?" Her flushed face was a mask of disbelief.

"You heard me."

"I did, but I doubted my ears. A man of your depth and perception must've realized that…"

His clamped fingers relaxed. "Realized…what exactly?"

"Must I say it out loud?"

"I think you'd better."

With a huff, she rolled her eyes. "Ranulf is just a friend. If I like anyone around here, 'tis *you*!"

He hesitated only an instant, long enough to absorb what she'd said. Then he grasped her arms, pulled her to him, and pressed his lips to hers.

Breaking free of his hold, she took his face between her hands and returned his kiss with passionate abandon. Her tongue took the lead. Her moan harmonized with the howling wind. She tasted of elderberries, ginger, and honey. Of lust and life.

Heat rushed through him, heightening every sense as he gave himself to the kiss. He ran his hands down her back to her hips and buttocks, pulling her hard against his swollen manhood.

Again, she moaned and ground her pelvis in a way that reminded him of her sensual dance in the solar that day, when she thought no one was looking. Slowly, her hand slid down his chest and stomach, all the way down to his...

He sucked in his breath. Though his tunic and breeches served as barriers, she squeezed his bulging member. He groaned in response.

"Argh!" Wide-eyed, she pushed away from him. "What are we doing? What am *I* doing?"

Shocked by both her bold behavior and hasty withdrawal, he stared at her rosy cheeks and lips. His body was afire from her touch, and he yearned to finish what they'd begun. But her question, her burning gaze, demanded an answer.

"I would've thought 'twas obvious." A foreign rasp altered his voice. He sounded nothing like himself.

"Obvious but unthinkable."

He slowed his breathing. "I've no wish to taint your virtue."

"And I've no wish to birth a babe out of wedlock."

Wedlock. Everyone expected him to wed Isobel, but...could he marry someone like Ardyth? He knew little of her family and fortune. The people loved her stories, and from all he'd observed, she was kind and generous. Yet there was something about her, unnamable and *different*. Even Giles had sensed it.

She was the most confusing woman he'd ever met. So she didn't need a man? Her actions just contradicted that. He himself had never felt such desire. And the thought of her married to another was...

"I cannot stay forever, Hugh."

Robert had given him a similar reminder. "Perhaps you can."

"As what? Your scribe?"

Why not? But no. He wanted more than that. Did she?

Thunder clapped outside and rumbled through the cave all around them.

She squared her shoulders. "I have…plans for my life."

"Plans?"

"You wouldn't understand if I told them to you. You wouldn't even believe me."

"You asked me not to underestimate you, and I shan't, no matter what you tell me."

Her eyes darkened as she held his gaze. Then she blinked and shook her head. "I'm sorry, Hugh. My plans for the future are private. I cannot share them with you."

It seemed his heart plummeted to the pit of his stomach. "The kiss we shared…it meant nothing to you?"

"Not nothing."

"But not enough."

She opened her mouth as if to speak, then clamped it shut.

Her silence pained his ears. As if to fill the void, thunder crashed again, louder than the waves upon the sand, yet far softer than Ardyth's intense stare and the rush of words he felt certain she *wanted* to say, but wouldn't. Why?

His stomach churned like the sea. "I'll leave you to your…plans. I wouldn't stay down here long. A storm blows nigh." He ripped his gaze from hers, turned his back, and strode from the cave.

Chapter Ten

Two stormy days followed before the sun reappeared in earnest. They might as well have been two weeks, for Ardyth dwelled in an emotional limbo from which there seemed no escape. Her attraction for Hugh was so intense, it was almost painful. She'd forgotten herself in the sea cave, and her roving hand had shown a will of its own.

No, that's not true, she thought as she, Lady Seacrest, Isobel, and Juliana exited the keep's forebuilding and started down the sunlit stairs to the bustling lower bailey. It was *her* will, *her* desire that urged her to reach below his belt and...

Heat flooded her face as she recalled the feel of him, rock hard, beneath her hand. Would a medieval lady have done that? Probably not. But then, she was neither medieval nor a lady. Therein lay the problem.

Who am I kidding? There are a buttload of problems!

Meg, the Ravenwood woman, had said she was destined to return to the future. But couldn't she make her own destiny? She'd been so certain of her path, so ready to earn her PhD and live the life of a professor...until the kiss. That one, blasted, incredible, toe-curling kiss!

Now she wasn't sure *what* she wanted. From his reaction, neither was Hugh. She'd asked him point-blank how she might remain at Seacrest.

As what? Your scribe?

And he'd said nothing. He just stared at her as if she'd erupted in scales and transformed into a fire-breathing dragon.

Did she want to stick around in the twelfth century as his scribe and lover, only to watch him marry a lady more suitable? Someone like Isobel or Juliana or some other woman who might steal his heart?

Absolutely not!

For the past two days, he had kept his distance. She'd seen him only at meals, during which Lady Seacrest sat between them, and he was overattentive to Isobel. Although his behavior irked her, it kept her libido in check. Still, the memory of their kiss kept popping up, like a song she couldn't get out of her head. The few instances when he *did* look her way, her breath caught in her throat, and she felt like a preteen suffering her first crush.

She was bound to see him now. They were all gathering in the courtyard to meet Isobel and Juliana's uncle, some high-up clergyman to whom Isobel had written the week before and whose invitation to stay Lady Seacrest had approved.

Hugh came into view. Ardyth's heart performed a maneuver that would've made her old gymnastics teacher proud.

Resplendent in red, he approached the newcomer with confident strides as they gathered round. "Archdeacon Dominy."

"Lord Seacrest." The clergyman's watchful, close-set eyes looked small in comparison to his full, ruddy cheeks. His white clothing was impeccable; his graying hair, not so much. The impressive buildup of grease would challenge even twentieth-century shampoo.

Lady Seacrest smiled graciously. "You're very welcome here, Archdeacon." She led the introductions.

When the archdeacon's gaze fell on Ardyth, his eyes narrowed. He looked her up and down and fingered his pectoral cross. Something within his beady eyes set her nerves on edge.

He returned his attention to Lillian. "Lady Seacrest, I hear Lord Harcourt's son is here. I knew his lordship and should like to have a word with Ranulf." His gaze slid to Hugh. "I would also speak with you, my lord, when you have a moment to spare."

"Of course," said Hugh, pokerfaced.

Ardyth frowned. She doubted Hugh welcomed the interview. What might they discuss? Almsgiving? His nieces' charms? Five ways to cleanse the soul without cleansing one's hair?

Isobel hurried forward. "Not now, though." With a glance toward Juliana, she ushered their uncle toward the keep. "I've much to tell you…"

Hugh watched the trio's departure, then turned to Lady Seacrest. "I'd like a word with you, Mother. In private."

"Certainly." With an arched brow, Lillian looked from him to Ardyth, then graced the latter with a reassuring smile.

Hugh cast Ardyth the briefest glance before turning away. "My lady."

"My lord." *At least you acknowledged my presence.*

She eyed his retreating form. His gleaming black hair. The broad shoulders beneath the red tunic. The spring in his step as he and Lillian headed toward the upper bailey.

Ardyth heaved a long sigh. Then she kicked an offending pebble out of her path and struck out in the opposite direction.

****

The morning waned as Hugh entered the castle's chapel. As always, the row of arched, stained glass windows and brightly painted murals cheered him, regardless of the man who stood beside Father Jacques in front of the altar.

Archdeacon Dominy simpered as Hugh approached them. "Ah, Lord Seacrest."

Hugh halted in front of the two men. "Archdeacon. Father Jacques."

Seacrest's aging priest wiped sweat from his brow. "My lord."

Dominy turned to the older man. "Prithee, leave us."

Jacques looked to Hugh, who gave him a nod. With bowed head, folded hands, and the air of a man who'd escaped the hangman's noose, the priest shuffled out of the chapel.

The archdeacon regarded Hugh. "Thank you for agreeing to meet me here. 'Tis best we converse in private."

"Why is that?"

"I wish to put you on your guard."

Hugh raised his eyebrows. "Against what?"

"Not what; whom." He began to pace before the altar. "My niece, Lady Isobel, wrote to me, begging my assistance. She feels a keen concern for your lordship and all of Seacrest, for she believes Lady Ardyth—"

"Lady Ardyth?" Hugh's pulse quickened.

Dominy stopped and nodded. "She's an ill influence. Her impudence…working as a scribe, swimming in the sea, entertaining the hall with songs and fanciful tales…these actions are highly suspect."

"Your niece's concern is unwarranted. Lady Ardyth's skill as a scribe is exceptional. Her songs and stories bring joy to all who hear them."

"You defend her."

"I do. As for the swimming, she does so in private."

Pious judgment flickered in the archdeacon's eyes. "Not always."

Hugh bristled. *Would Isobel's mouth were bolted like a batten door!* "What are you insinuating?"

"I insinuate naught. I state openly that you swam with her ladyship earlier this week."

"It may have escaped your notice, Archdeacon, but I am free to do whatever I please on my own estate."

"But such freedoms should not extend to Lady—"

"Would you object if I swam with your niece?"

Dominy pressed his thin lips together. "That is not the issue. My niece fears Lady Ardyth has bewitched you."

There'd been moments when Hugh wondered the same thing, but not in terms of actual witchery. "Lady Ardyth is no more a witch than your nieces, or my mother, for that matter."

The archdeacon's expression soured. "As with Eve herself, all women are called to sin, to use those wicked wiles that entice righteous men to stray from God's will."

"What? Has someone led *you* astray?"

Dominy's dark eyes flared. He fondled his pectoral cross, and it seemed to calm him. "We are not discussing me. Lady Ardyth's deeds give me pause, and that should not be taken lightly. I'm told she aligns herself with the owl, a creature with evil tendencies."

"'Tis but a term of endearment her father gave her."

"Why would he give it if not for some suspicion of her character? Owls revel in darkness."

"But they're superb hunters of vermin." Hugh grinned inwardly. With his beady eyes and pinched mouth, the archdeacon looked rather like a rat himself.

"Be that as it may, you must watch yourself. The future Lady Seacrest must be a lady of quality, proper and devout."

"Like Lady Isobel?"

"Precisely."

What gall! He might be a man of the cloth, but his manner, tone, and advice were ranker than a gongpit.

"You may thank Lady Isobel for her concern, Archdeacon, but in such matters, I shall heed my *own* counsel and no one else's. Good day to you." He swung around and marched toward the exit.

"Lord Seacrest!"

Hugh ignored the archdeacon and passed through the archway to freedom. His mind awhirl, he hurried down the stairs.

Isobel had stirred up trouble, and Ardyth...perhaps he'd been wrong to ignore her the past two days. Snubbing her was one of the hardest things he'd ever done, though it offered him a measure of protection from her charms. God's bones, but she was hard to read! What exactly were her intentions? What plans were so important to her?

Plans be damned! That glorious kiss in the sea cave *had* to mean something. A woman didn't grab a man's member for naught!

No one can tell me whom I should or shouldn't court. Not the archdeacon. Not Isobel. His heart beat faster, and he smiled. *Not even Ardyth.*

Chapter Eleven

At supper that night, Hugh was all politeness. Ardyth welcomed the change but wondered what had caused it. Lillian, who sat between them at table, smiled a lot and seemed content to sit back and allow the two of them to converse freely about history and Seacrest's inhabitants over their meal of poached fowl and pudding.

Less pleased were Isobel and Dominy, whose competing scowls were like a chorus of disapproval. Ignoring their ill humor, Juliana focused adoring, puppy-dog eyes on Ranulf. The goliard's inflammatory songs about the Church deepened the archdeacon's frown but brought an uncharacteristic grin to Giles's face. Perhaps Dominy's ire amused the minstrel, for he sang just two songs about the Seacrest treasure, then let Ranulf perform for the remainder of the meal.

After supper, it was Ardyth's turn to entertain. She sang a few tunes from *The Sound of Music* but bowed out of story time. Her refusal prompted sighs of disappointment from many in the hall, but her mind was too full of Hugh to plot and perform a spellbinding tale. He'd listened to her singing with bright eyes and vanished from the gallery the instant she finished.

Where'd he go? Is he coming down here? Her heart did a jig.

Ranulf rushed up to her. "Beautiful songs as

always, my lady."

"Thank you. I enjoyed yours too, as did Lady Juliana."

"Lady Juliana?"

"Aye. She relishes all your performances, and I'm certain she'd like to know what inspires you. If you want to speak to her about it, she's right over there."

"Oh?" He followed her gaze to one of the dormant fireplaces, in front of which Juliana and Isobel chatted animatedly. "Perhaps I will…"

Ardyth smiled. *Matchmaker, matchmaker, make me a match.*

"Ranulf," a gruff male voice sounded behind her.

The skin on the back of her neck crawled. She turned.

Archdeacon Dominy. Standing way too close for comfort.

"Good evening," Ranulf said calmly.

"I must speak with you. Your blatant disregard for—"

"Forgive me, Archdeacon, but there's a matter of great importance I must see to." The goliard skipped out of trouble and made a beeline for Juliana.

Good for you, Ardyth thought as he hurried away. Then she groaned inside. *Bad for me.*

"Lady Ardyth," Dominy said in a smoother tone. "You have quite the voice."

She fought a frown. His compliment sounded sincere, and yet…oily. "Thank you, Archdeacon."

"I never would've expected so heavenly a sound to come from…" He reached a hand toward her arm.

She took a step backward, avoiding his touch. "From a woman?"

124

He caressed the cross at his breast. "You read my thoughts."

"'Twas only a guess."

"An unnaturally accurate one." His gaze transfixed, he stepped closer. His hand slipped off the cross, seeking her arm once more, and the fingers made contact.

She jerked her arm away. "Touch me again and you might not have a hand to stroke your...cross."

He dropped his hand, and his ruddy complexion darkened further. "You should address me with respect. I'm an archdeacon."

"You're a fop if you think your title will garner respect your actions do not earn."

His dark eyes widened. "Insufferable—"

"A word, my lady." Hugh was suddenly at her side.

Relief flowed through her, and excitement followed on its heels as she turned to face him. "Only a word? Why so modest? Let's have a whole conversation. Someplace calm, where we can enjoy a leisurely stroll."

His gray eyes twinkled. "I'm to meet my mother in the solar soon, but I have time for a stroll. In the lower bailey?"

"Sounds perfect."

"Excuse us, Archdeacon."

They left Dominy open-mouthed and alone, but not for long. He strode to the table where Giles was sitting and plopped down beside him on the bench.

What could they have to talk about? Perhaps they'd swap complaints about Ranulf.

Or maybe they'll have a staring contest, she thought with a grin. *A battle royale to see which scowl outlasts the other.* Both men were champs, as far as she was concerned, but Isobel could definitely give them a run for their money.

Not that it mattered. What *did* matter was Hugh and this unexpected chance to spend time with him. Side by side, they cleared a path through the crowded hall and quieter waiting room, then entered the forebuilding, with its succession of high arches.

Hugh slowed his stride but carried on toward the exit. "I heard what you said to the archdeacon."

"Are you going to scold me?"

"No."

"Good, because I'm not sorry for what I said. I don't know how other women have dealt with his attentions, but if he wants to draw breath, he'd better not bother me again."

He chuckled as they started down the broad steps. "Heaven help him if he does!"

"Ah, so you've learned not to underestimate me." *That's one small step for woman; one giant leap for womankind.*

"I suppose I have, but don't underrate *him* either." They reached the bailey floor and continued walking in the direction of the mill. "He believes you're a bad influence on Seacrest."

"He hardly knows me. How would he…" The question trailed off as realization dawned. "Lady Isobel, of course. That's why she invited him."

"And why he asked to speak with me earlier."

"To warn you against me?"

"Aye."

She arched an eyebrow. "And what say *you*? Am I a bad influence?"

"Need you ask?"

"Well, aye. I cannot read your mind, and in the whole of Seacrest's history, I'm still a newcomer. Almost a stranger."

He stopped in front of the large barn that served as the granary. She also halted and scanned the bailey, basking in the soft evening light and the hush which had settled over the land. She would miss the stillness, the slower pace of life, when she returned to her own time.

She longed to confide in Hugh: about her true identity, the 1980s, everything! She'd come close to dropping the bomb in the sea cave after the ill-fated kiss but caught herself in the nick of time. A good thing, too. He would've thought she was crazy, and she wouldn't have blamed him one bit.

If only she *could* tell him. She sighed, and her heart ached as she turned to him.

A warm breeze riffled his hair, and his eyes seemed to bore into her soul. "You're no stranger, Ardyth."

Her name on his tongue was like an aphrodisiac. Her heart fluttered and quickened its pace. Heat crept up her neck and into her face, and she felt wet between the legs.

He took a step closer. "The other day, you said I prized Lady Isobel's opinion over yours, but you were mistaken."

"Oh? Then why did you ignore me the past two days?"

"Why do *you* keep your plans for the future a secret?"

"One has nothing to do with the other."

"Hasn't it?"

Thwack!

She jumped. The sound came from inside the granary. "What was that?"

With a frown, Hugh glanced at the building, then started up the ramp toward the door. She followed close behind him.

The spacious interior was quiet, as it should be this time of night. Sacks of threshed grain, barley, and rye crowded both the main floor and loft. A tarp-covered cart stood close to the door. All was still until…

The velvety flap of near-silent wings ruffled the air above them. A barn owl glided down from the loft and landed on a lower beam.

She smiled up at it. "'Tis *you* we heard!"

Hugh moved closer. "This might be the same creature whose feather became your quill."

"Do you come hither often?"

"On occasion, in the evenings. 'Tis peaceful, and I find it satisfying to stand amid the stores that feed all of Seacrest."

The owl's gaze moved back and forth between them, then settled on Ardyth.

Again, she smiled. "Sweet owl, if you *did* lend a feather for my pen, thank you." She stared into its dark eyes, and the medieval symbolism associated with the raptor leapt to mind. "How could anyone think you're evil?"

"How could anyone think *you* are?"

The tenderness and depth of emotion in Hugh's voice struck her unawares. She lowered her gaze to his, which was every bit as dark and inviting as the owl's.

"Ardyth."

"Hugh." He was a breath away.

"My lord!" Bertram the steward burst into the granary. "Forgive my intrusion, but there's been another robbery."

Hugh's brow puckered as he regarded the muscular, middle-aged seneschal. "Wine again?"

Bertram nodded. "That makes four thefts in less than a fortnight, according to the butler."

"I shall speak with him directly." He turned to her. "My lady, I regret—"

"Don't say another word, my lord. I understand completely." *And I'd like a word with someone myself.*

****

A short while later, Hugh exited the wine cellar and climbed the steps with Bertram. "I want a guard in the cellar and another in the buttery at all times."

"Aye, my lord."

"And I want a list of all servants hired within the past few weeks."

"I'll see to it."

"At least the spices appear untouched."

"A blessing indeed."

They reached the floor above and carried on past the buttery and pantry. A blond page, no older than ten, scurried around the corner and stopped them in their tracks.

"Hail to your lordship." The boy handed Hugh a bit of folded parchment. "A message from Lady Ardyth."

Hugh's eyes widened. "Lady Ardyth?"

"Aye, my lord."

"Thank you, Ancelot. You may go."

The boy scampered off, and Hugh opened the parchment. The script looked different from Ardyth's formal hand, but that was to be expected.

"*Meet me in the granary.*"

"The granary?" His pulse quickened. He'd been about to kiss her when Bertram interrupted them there; she must've known it. Mayhap she wanted what had been denied her.

He was eager to oblige. His mother awaited him in the solar, but she could wait a little longer.

"Thank you, Bertram. We'll resume our inquiry on the morrow."

"Aye, my lord."

He hastened out of the keep, through the bailey, and up the ramp to the granary, then pushed open the door. Parchment in hand, he scanned the building.

Mountains of grain. The same cart as before. But no Ardyth.

With furrowed brow, he approached the cart and pulled back the cloth to examine its contents. Fishing spears. Baskets. Rope, coiled in a corner like a snake.

His frown deepened. *Fishing gear? Why would—*

Pain struck the back of his head. Darkness enclosed him.

Chapter Twelve

After a lengthy, introspective walk through the lower and upper baileys, Ardyth strode with purpose into the chamber she shared with Juliana and Isobel. Only the latter was present, lounging on the larger mattress in her chemise and combing out her long, brown hair.

All too aware of the numerous ears just outside in the hall, Ardyth spoke in a low voice. "You must truly hate me to send your archdeacon of an uncle to besmirch my character."

The comb stilled. "Whatever do you mean?"

"You know perfectly well my meaning. You invited him to Seacrest to turn his lordship against me."

"You do think highly of yourself to imagine—"

"I imagine naught. I know. You're determined to do whatever it takes to marry Lord Seacrest."

Isobel's chin jutted out. "I object to this—"

"It didn't work, by the way. His lordship told me everything."

She dropped the comb, and it thumped onto the mattress. "Did he now?"

"Oh, he did. He's far too strong a man to accept another's counsel on such matters, especially when that counsel vilifies an innocent person."

"Innocent? Ha! You've thrown your dice in his direction since the day you arrived!"

"Not true."

"By God's nails, I say it is!"

"Quiet down, Isobel!" Juliana hurried into the room. "Do you want everyone to hear?"

Isobel's eyes flared. "Where have *you* been?"

Juliana laced her fingers together. Her face fairly glowed. "With Ranulf."

"All this time?"

Juliana shrugged. "Most of it."

"Doing what, pray?"

"Talking."

Isobel gave her a sideways look. "Hmm." She returned her attention to Ardyth. "Lord Seacrest belongs with me."

Ardyth folded her arms. "If that is so, you have nothing to fear from me."

"She has a point," Juliana said.

Isobel glared at her sister. "I should've expected you to take her part."

"Why? Because she's been kind to me? To *us*?"

"Juliana the jester! Open your eyes. A viper's kindness we can do without."

"Ladies." Lillian stood in the doorway. "I beg you would forgive the intrusion, but I must speak with Lady Ardyth."

"Of course," said Ardyth, relieved to escape the cramped quarters and Isobel's wrath. She followed Lady Seacrest out of the chamber and through the hall, where most of the servants were settling onto pallets, benches, and the floor to sleep.

"After your performance tonight," Lillian murmured, "did you see Lord Seacrest?"

"I did."

"He told me he would speak with you and then meet me in the solar. We were to plan our trip to Ravenwood, to see my first grandchild once 'tis born, but…"

A knot formed in Ardyth's stomach. Something was wrong; she could hear it in Lillian's voice. "What?"

"He never came. My son has faults enough, but he keeps his promises. Where did you last see him?"

"The granary. Bertram came in and reported trouble in the buttery. Stolen wine, apparently. They went off to look into the matter."

"Hmm. Might they still be in the buttery? Or perhaps the wine cellar?"

"'Twas a good while ago." Without a watch, she couldn't be sure, but she guessed at least an hour. "I'd imagine Bertram is in his chamber now. We should check with him."

Lillian nodded. "Good idea."

A growing sense of urgency carried them to the door of the steward's chamber. Lillian knocked three times.

The door creaked open, and a tousle-haired Bertram scratched his head. "Lady Seacrest?"

"Have you any idea where his lordship is?"

"Not this moment." Bertram focused his weary gaze on Ardyth. "Wasn't he with you?"

"Me?"

"Aye. Right after we left the cellar, a page gave him your note."

Lillian turned to her. "Note?"

Ardyth shrugged. "This is the first I've heard of it."

Bertram frowned. "You didn't send his lordship a

message?"

"Absolutely not."

Again, he scratched his head. "Curious."

"I don't like the idea of someone pretending to be me."

"Neither do I." Lillian twisted her hands. "Bertram, what was the message?"

"I didn't read it. But his lordship mentioned the granary before he hurried off."

Lillian's determined glance met and matched Ardyth's. "Right. To the granary."

"Shall I come too?" Bertram offered.

"No. Stay here, and if his lordship should appear, tell him whither we've gone."

"Of course, my lady."

The women scurried through the twilit bailey to the granary, and Ardyth darted inside.

"Hugh?"

No answer. No Hugh.

No cart, she thought, frowning at the spot near the door where it had stood.

Lillian raised her eyebrows. "You call him by his given name?"

"I do when we're alone, and he calls me by mine as well."

A champagne-colored scrap on the ground caught her eye, and she stooped to pick it up. " 'Meet me in the granary,' " she read aloud, then passed the note to Lillian. "He must've dropped it."

"We need to find the page who delivered it."

"Aye, but first we need to find Hugh. Someone lured him hither, and if I'm not mistaken, took him by force."

Lillian pressed a hand to her chest. "Blessed Virgin! How do you know?"

"'Tis only a guess. But he dropped the paper, which I cannot imagine he'd do unless caught off-guard, and a cart with cloth enough to cover it was here before but is now missing. Someone might've transported him in it."

Screech!

They both started, then looked up. A barn owl perched on an overhead beam.

"I trow he's the same owl that was here before." Tilting her head to the side, Ardyth spoke directly to him. "Did you see something which can help us?"

She stared into the bird's eyes. So dark. Fathomless. Eternal.

The sea cave. Go by way of the secret passage.

She gasped. Had the words actually come from the owl? When she first arrived in this time, little Freya told her those of the Nightshade and Ravenwood lines had special gifts. Could communicating with animals be one of them? It had never happened before.

"What is it?" Lillian demanded.

"This will sound strange…in fact, completely mad…but I think the owl just answered my question. You know the secret tunnel down to the sea cave?"

The older woman's wrinkled brow smoothed. "I do, but…how do *you*?"

"Hugh showed it to me. We must use it now."

"Is Hugh in the cave?"

"Let's find out."

They raced to the solar, and Lillian grabbed a lighted torch from the wall. Stepping behind the unicorn screen, they lifted the trapdoor and descended the steps. They followed the cold, humid passage all the way to the opening and the seven-foot-high rock which stuck out from the cliff. The wind lashed them, extinguishing the torch, and the waves crashed far below.

Lillian tossed the torch into the tunnel and laid a hand on the tall rock. "The boys called this the Rock Man when they were younger." Fear darkened her eyes. "What if someone has hurt him? What if…"

Ardyth placed a comforting hand on the woman's shoulder. "Calm yourself, my lady. I trust he's well." *He has to be!*

They hurried along the ledge to the mouth of the sea cave and peered inside. Ardyth's stomach dropped, and a surge of nausea hit her.

His head hung low, Hugh sat on the distant ledge, with the three tunnels behind him. Rope cinched his ankles together, and his hands, presumably tied, were behind his back. Two men—one lanky, the other hulking—stood before him. The first spoke in a threatening tone; because the receding tide was still high, the slurp and splash of water resonated within the cave and muddled his words.

Hugh lifted his head and uttered a low reply.

Her heart beat faster. *He's alive, and conscious! Thank God!*

The second, heavier man raised a dagger and waved it in the air. Slowly, he positioned the blade at Hugh's throat.

Lillian gasped. Ardyth grabbed her arm and pulled her back behind the cover of rock.

"Forgive me, my lady, but they mustn't see us."

"But we must help him!"

"Agreed. Give me a moment to think." Memories from a self-defense class and of Giles's songs swirled in her mind and interwove to form a plan. Not a great one, but it would have to suffice.

She pulled off her boots and stockings, then donned the shoes again. Setting the stockings aside, she searched the ground, snatched a rock the size of a large onion, and handed it to Lady Seacrest. "If I knock a man to the ground, can you hit him over the head with this?"

Lillian's eyes widened. Then she nodded.

"Good. Go hide in the tunnel and be ready!"

Ardyth cupped her hands around her mouth to magnify the sound and sang the "ah" vowel in a haunting, ethereal tune. With any luck, the thugs would think she was one of the ghosts or fairies Giles had invented, and one would come to investigate.

Before long, the larger of the two trod around the corner and stopped short at the sight of her. "What are you doing here?"

Lifting her skirts, she kicked upward between his legs, and her shin slammed into his groin. He doubled over, and she punched him in the temple. "Now!" As he fell to the ground, one hand right at the edge of the cliff, Lillian lunged toward him and struck his head with the rock. After that, he lay silent and still.

Her heart pounding, Ardyth bound his ankles with one stocking, then tied up his hands with the other. She seized his dagger and looked heavenward in a silent prayer. *One down; one to go. Please help me!*

Lillian wiped the sweat from her brow. "What now?"

"Does anyone else in Seacrest know of the secret

passage?"

"Only Bertram."

"All right. Go and fetch him."

"What will you do?"

She thought for a moment. "I doubt the other man will leave Hugh alone, so I'll have to sneak down and stop him somehow. Oh…if you could give me your stockings…"

"Of course." Lillian doffed her slippers and stockings and handed the latter to Ardyth. "Do be careful, my dear."

The warmth in Lillian's voice bolstered Ardyth's courage. "I will. Now, hurry!" Stockings in one hand and the dagger gripped in the other, she stepped over the first guy and stole into the cave.

The other brute was talking to Hugh, but as before, the swish of the ocean garbled his words. Her heart in her throat, she crept down along the cave's ledge.

When she was halfway down, Hugh glanced her way. His eyes widened, but the next instant, his gaze shot back to his captor. She knew instinctively he didn't want to give her away, and now *he* knew help was here. If she didn't blow it!

Slow and steady, she thought, inching closer. A few seconds more, and the villain's peripheral vision might detect her.

"Degarre!" he shouted without turning. "What did you find?"

Almost there! At most, eight yards away.

"Degarre, you mumblecrust, why are you always so…" He turned and did a double take. Then he leered at her. "What have we here?"

Hugh kicked both feet together, striking the man's

legs and knocking him off balance. The thug fell backward, landing on the wet sand twenty feet below. "Ah! My leg!" Said leg was bent at an unnatural angle.

"Ardyth!" Hugh's voice sounded husky.

She rushed toward him and took his handsome face in her hands. The stubble on his cheeks tickled her palms. "Are you hurt?"

He gave her a half-smile that seemed born of surprise and gratitude. "My head aches, but I'll be fine." He looked beyond her, toward the mouth of the cave. "Where's the other one?"

"Bound and unconscious up on the cliff walk." She attempted to cut the rope at his wrists with the dagger.

"How did you manage that?"

"I thought you were done underestimating me."

"I thought I was too, but…this is incredible!"

She grinned but lost her humor as she continued to fight the rope. "Your mother helped, too."

"My mother?"

She huffed. "I thought daggers were supposed to be sharp." At last, the blade did its job. "There! Finally!"

He wriggled his free hands. "Give me the dagger."

She handed him the weapon, and he worked on his other bond. The crook below cried out in pain once more.

She winced. "I think he broke his leg, so he won't escape. What did they want anyway?"

His expression darkened. "The location of the Seacrest treasure."

"Hmph. By the way, I did *not* write the note that sent you to the granary."

"I gathered as much." He freed his feet and stood. "How did you learn of it?"

"From Bertram. Actually, he should be here any moment."

"How did you know I was here?"

She hesitated. "I know I keep saying this, but you wouldn't believe me if I told you."

All at once, the steward and Lady Seacrest dashed into the cave and hurried down the ledge toward them.

Lillian breathed a sigh of relief and hugged her son. "God be praised!"

Hugh pulled back and gave her a wry smile. "I hear *you* had a hand in it. And Lady Ardyth, of course."

Lillian clapped her hands together. "Indeed! You should've seen her ladyship. She fought as well as ever a man did."

He cocked an eyebrow. "Oh?"

Heat flooded Ardyth's face. "I only did what was necessary."

Lillian put a gentle hand on her back. "What's necessary now is that you get some rest."

Bertram peered down at the injured man, then averted his gaze and shook his head. "My lord, I think it best we keep this incident quiet. We don't want to start a panic."

Hugh nodded. "I agree."

Lillian gave the villain a hard look. "I'll alert the jailer and tell him to stay silent as well. Bertram, help his lordship get these fat-kidneyed knaves up to the keep and into the dungeon, where they belong."

****

The next morning, Hugh and Bertram strode through the lower bailey in search of young Ancelot. The sun shone bright, and not a single body was idle.

The steward heaved an impatient sigh. "If only

those dirty rotters could tell us who hired them. If they'd but seen his face…"

"'Twas clever of him to wear the masked hood of a leper."

"And to pay them with pilfered wine until he could give them their share of the supposed treasure. Your hunch about checking the records for recent hires was a good one."

"A carter and a fisherman. Perfect covers for men who needed to haul something…namely me…down to the beach."

"And haul nonexistent riches out of the cave."

Hugh nodded. "'Tis time I stopped Giles from singing those songs. Ah, here we are."

The boyish whoops of pages mixed with the clatters and clangs of squires honing their skills in swordplay. A handful of squires practiced archery. One page brandished a wooden sword against an obliging pole, and another tilted a blunt-tipped lance while sitting atop a wooden horse on wheels, pulled along by two other pages. Three more pages—one, the golden-haired Ancelot—cleaned rust from chain mail by rolling it in barrels of sand.

"Ancelot," Hugh called.

The boy looked up and abandoned his barrel to stand before the baron and his steward. "My lord?"

"The message you handed me last night…who gave it to you?"

The page's brow crinkled. "One of the carters. A big man, he is."

"Was anyone with him?"

"No, he was alone. He gave me a sweetmeat and told me the note from Lady Ardyth must be delivered straightaway."

"I see. Thank you, Ancelot. You may return to your duties."

"Aye, my lord." He skipped back to rejoin the others.

Bertram crossed his arms. "Well, that confirms what the knaves said about the note."

"It does, and according to the one called Degarre, the masked man wrote it."

"A learned man, then." The steward's eyes widened. "And he's here at Seacrest."

"Quite." Hugh rubbed his newly shaven jaw. "I've been thinking...they first met him at a tavern in York, where he encouraged them to seek work here. Who else hails from York? A man of learning, who has just arrived..."

Bertram reflected for a moment, then slowly turned his head toward his lord. "Archdeacon Dominy? But...but he's a man of God!"

Hugh frowned, his gaze trained on a squire whose arrow had just hit its mark. "Aye. A slippery one."

Chapter Thirteen

Ardyth rambled through the upper bailey with Juliana. The changeful morning breeze brought the varied scents of flowers, herbs, and the briny water below, one after the other. The high-pitched call of gulls punctuated the song of the sea, which wrapped around them and the garden's fragrant beauty.

Juliana sighed with contentment. "Whatever you said to Ranulf yesternight, thank you."

Ardyth made a dismissive gesture. "I merely pointed him in your direction. What happened after that, you owe entirely to your own charms."

Juliana's cheeks turned as pink as the roses at her feet. "I'll admit, he mentioned a fair few of them. He actually said, 'Your hair is the color of sweet, dark honey.'"

"I'd agree with that statement."

"As for *his* looks…those dark eyes and the cleft in his chin…" She heaved a musical sigh. "They make me feel rather giddy."

"I quite understand."

Without warning, Juliana's face fell. "I doubt my uncle would approve. He hardly approves of *me*."

I doubt he approves of Mother Mary herself. She cleared her throat. "What sort of man is your uncle, really?"

"Devout. Demanding. Whenever he came to visit, I

did my best to avoid him. He's a bore!"

And a boor to boot! Dominy was repulsive. But did he have the makings of a criminal?

Juliana pushed a wandering strand of hair behind her ear. "I trow his goal is the same as my sister's: to see Lord Seacrest married to her." She gave Ardyth a rueful smile. "Poor Isobel! She hates competition, and she's been such a windsucker since your arrival. But you mustn't take it personally. She'd be jealous of anyone who presented a threat."

"And you think I do?"

"I know it. Isobel does, too."

A brooding Ranulf stalked through the decorative arch in the stone wall that separated the two baileys. As soon as he spotted them, his frown transformed into a smile.

"Lady Juliana, Lady Ardyth. What do you here on so fine a morning?"

Juliana studied his face. "It didn't look so fine a moment ago. What troubles you?"

He gave her an appreciative look. "Beautiful, kind, *and* insightful. Take care, or I may lose my heart!"

Again, she blushed. "Tell me, what cause have you to frown?"

"Two individuals who are in a foul mood this morrow. One is your uncle."

"'Tisn't unusual."

"Perhaps not, but it does present a problem, especially where we're concerned. He thinks poorly of me, I'm afraid."

Ardyth gave him a compassionate smile. "He thinks poorly of many. But mayhap, if you tempered your songs a bit...so they're less critical of the

Church…"

He fingered the cleft in his chin. "Aye. That might be a start. He did know my father as well. Years ago, of course, but if I remind him of those days, he might view me with a kinder eye."

Juliana beamed at him. "Anything is possible." She turned to Ardyth. "Isn't that right?"

"Absolutely." *Even time travel, for crying out loud!* She regarded Ranulf. "Who else is in a foul mood?"

"Giles. Not that there's aught strange about that, but today there's real cause for his distemper. Lord Seacrest told him to stop singing about the treasure. I wonder why?"

Ardyth wanted to confide in them about Hugh's recent ordeal but thought better of it. "Perhaps he's tired of Giles spreading falsehoods."

Ranulf raised an eyebrow. "Or perhaps he wants to keep the treasure safe for future generations."

"Who could blame his lordship?" Juliana chimed in. "If indeed that be true."

The goliard turned to Ardyth. "While we're on the subject of his lordship, shouldn't you be with him, working on the family history?"

"I should." She grinned. *And three's a crowd. I get it!* "I'll leave you to enjoy each other's company. Until later!"

She hurried down the garden path, up the wooden stairs, and into the keep, not stopping until she reached the solar's entrance. Inside, Hugh stood next to her writing desk with his back turned. He was staring at the open window.

"Hugh?"

He turned and gave her a preoccupied smile. His

gray tunic intensified the gray of his eyes. "Come in."

She entered the room and halted in front of him. "How is your head?"

"Much improved, thank you."

"I'm glad to hear it. Tell me, before I came, what were your thoughts?"

He linked his hands behind him. "I was trying to make sense of what happened last night."

"I guessed as much. You questioned the prisoners?"

"I did."

"What did you learn?"

He crossed to the empty fireplace. "Ardyth, I've no wish to involve you in—"

"I'm already involved. I gave one of them a kick and a punch he won't soon forget, and they used *my name* to get to you."

He faced her again. "They used it, but they didn't write it. In fact, neither of them can read."

"Then who *did* write the note?"

"A man they met in York."

"Can they identify him?"

He shook his head. "They never saw his face."

"How convenient."

"Quite." He returned to the desk and picked up the quill he'd made for her. His long fingers stroked the soft, furry end of the pen.

Dear God, what if he stroked me *like that?* Heat streamed through her body, and she licked her lips. *Think of something else, anything else! He mentioned York. Yeah, York.* "Doesn't Archdeacon Dominy live in York?"

Hugh replaced the quill pen. "He does, but so do

Isobel and Juliana...ordinarily. Ranulf's family also hails from York. Even Giles has kin there."

"Well, that helps a lot." She couldn't soften the sarcasm in her voice, but at least she'd regained her composure.

"And you, Ardyth?" His gaze held hers. "Where is *your* home?"

Right here. With you. She blinked and stemmed the rising tide of emotion so she could offer an intelligible reply. Although she longed to tell him the truth about her circumstances, she didn't dare. "The North, near Nihtscua."

"I hear the frustration in your voice. I, too, hoped to learn more from the prisoners."

With a sigh, she ran her hand along the top of a high-backed chair. "Luckily, we disappointed the person in charge. His men...or her men—"

"Her?"

She held up her hands. "Very well, *his* men are in the dungeon, and the treasure remains hidden."

"There is no treasure."

"You're certain of that?"

"I am."

A string of memories struck home. "I just realized...several times while we were working in here together, I heard shuffling outside the door. Could it have been one of those men, eavesdropping to see if you mentioned treasure as part of the family history?"

"'Tis possible."

"And just as possible the person who hired them is no longer in York but right here within these walls."

"He must be, particularly in light of the fake message and the stolen wine, which he used to satisfy the prisoners until he could offer them a more substantial reward." His brow furrowed. "We may learn more when he targets me again."

Her stomach dropped as if she rode a rollercoaster, just as it had when she saw him tied in the cave with the dagger at his throat. Terror filled her as she imagined what might've happened if the blade had struck home. She'd admitted something to herself last night, as she lay on her mattress listening to Juliana's snores and Isobel's deep, even breathing—she was falling in love with Hugh.

Falling? No, she had fallen and now landed with a thud.

I love him.

She'd had a few boyfriends, John being the most recent, but she'd never loved them. Now the deed was done, and there was nothing she could do to change it.

Hugh took a step toward her. "Let's set our work aside and spend the day away from Seacrest. Away from everything. What say you?"

She gazed into his soulful, steel-gray eyes. He was the lonely boy, trapped by duty and a lifetime of responsibility, while his brothers escaped to make their own lives and become best friends. He was also the man of honor and wit, who stole her breath with each devastating smile. And yes, he was the kindred spirit who cherished history and demanded true love from his future mate.

She bestowed on him her brightest smile. "I say aye."

****

Hugh reined in his black stallion next to the burbling river. Ardyth, riding astride her brown palfrey, did the same. The hem of her violet gown rode too, all the way up to her knees, giving him a good view of a beautifully shaped, stockinged calf. The wooded valley was almost entirely surrounded by steep banks which formed a natural barrier to the world outside, and that was fine with him. He craved time alone with her. She filled so completely the lonely void created by his brothers' leaving, and he wanted to learn everything he could about her.

He dismounted and turned to help her down, but she'd already alighted on her own. Breathing deeply of the fresh, saltless air, he tied the horses to a low-hanging branch and grabbed the wineskin and bag of food Aubert had packed for them. "Hungry?"

She lifted a hand to her belly. "Starved! What did you bring?"

"In honor of the first time we ate in private, I had Aubert make something like your sand-wich."

"You remembered the word!"

"I did, but how do you refer to more than one of them?"

"Sandwiches."

"Sand-wich-es. He made two. Duck and cheese this time, with the uncooked lettuce again."

"So you *did* like the lettuce! It adds a nice crunch."

"That it does. Shall we sit?" He motioned to a soft patch of grass near the river's edge, and they sat down.

"What did you bring to drink?"

"Spiced wine." He handed her a sandwich, then took a bite of his own.

"M-m," she hummed, her mouth full of the same goodness that filled his own. "Heaven. Particularly the cheese."

"You share my passion for food."

"I never met a cheese I didn't like."

He burst out laughing.

Her brow crinkled. "What?"

"'Twas your choice of words. I've never heard anyone speak of food as though 'twere a person."

"Oh, I have a deep admiration and affection for cheese."

He grinned. *It seems I have a rival for your affections.* "As have I."

They shared drink from the wineskin. Every time he took a draught, he reveled in the fact his mouth touched the same spout as hers. *Oh, to kiss those lips again!* He would do it, when the time was right.

The sparkling water accompanied their meal with soothing gurgles and murmurs. Birdsong added harmony, and Hugh basked in a warm and radiant peace he hadn't felt for quite some time. All his cares were back at Seacrest. Here and now, in this place, he was free.

When food and drink were gone, he lay on his side facing her, propped up on one elbow. Lovelier than ever, Ardyth stared at the river with a faraway look in her eyes. She appeared content, but he couldn't be sure.

Suddenly, her brow puckered. "Hugh…"

"Aye?"

"Why are you convinced there's no treasure?"

"Because I know the truth of how the rumor started." He plucked a blade of grass from the ground and rubbed it between his fingers. "I trust my mother told you what happened with the shipwreck…that my father saved her life."

"She did."

"Afterward, when he spoke of his 'treasure beyond compare,' he meant *her*."

Ardyth's brown eyes widened. "Lady Seacrest was the treasure?"

"She was. Others simply mistook his words."

"That's some mistake! And now it has brought danger to your door."

"Indeed." He smiled. "You do have a unique way of putting things."

"Thank you…I think."

He dropped the blade of grass and sat up. "Now you must tell me…how did you know to look for me in the cave last night?"

She bit her luscious lower lip, then gave him a curt nod, as if she'd reached a decision. "Very well, I'll tell you. Bertram told us you mentioned the granary after reading the note, so we went thither. The owl you and I saw earlier was still there. I don't know what made me do it, but I asked him for help. And then, as I stared into his eyes, I got an answer. 'Twas as if he planted the words in my mind: 'the sea cave…go by way of the secret passage.' "

"You actually heard a voice?"

"'Tis woodness, I know, but I swear to you, I heard a male voice. Now that I think of it, it almost sounded like…no. That's impossible."

He frowned. "What is it?"

"Naught. I'm sure I'm wrong. Anyway, we found you, and the rest you know."

"Not in full. You said you kicked and punched the man called Degarre. I would I'd seen you."

She jumped to her feet. "I'll show you now, if you'd like. I promise to be gentle."

A wicked grin spread across her face. God's teeth, but she was alluring!

He stood, all too aware of his stiff manhood. "Show me."

She stepped closer. "I kicked here…" Swiftly, she lifted her leg between his, thankfully stopping short of the obvious goal. "…and he bent forward." Grasping his shoulders, she made him fold over at the waist. "Then I punched him right here." Her fist tapped his temple. "He fell to the ground, and your mother hit him over the head with a rock. Then I tied his hands and feet with my stockings."

He whistled as he straightened. "Pray, remind me not to anger you in future."

Again, she grinned. "Fear not. You're safe with me."

"Am I?" He inched closer, and an invisible cloak of intimacy wrapped around them.

Her smile disappeared, and her eyes darkened in a subtle yet soulful invitation. "Always."

He lowered his head and kissed her tenderly, encircling her waist with his hands. Her hands slipped up his chest to his neck, and her fingers combed through his hair, tugging, caressing, proving irrefutably that she desired him as he did her. With a deep moan, he pulled her against his throbbing member and plunged his tongue into her sweet mouth.

The kiss grew heated, hungry. His hands squeezed her breasts, her buttocks. He couldn't get enough of her mouth, her curves, the mingled scent of her hair and sweat. All the while, her honeyed sighs urged him onward.

But we are unwed, our future undecided. Can I ask

this of her?

He tore his mouth from hers. "Ardyth, I would know every inch of you."

Her eyes were pools of passion. "I want that too." She squeezed her eyes shut. "But…"

He kissed her forehead. "I'm listening."

Her eyes opened and seemed to plead for understanding. "I don't want a child out of wedlock."

Sympathy fought with his need for her. "I can appreciate that." His arms tightened around her waist. "There are…*other* ways we could enjoy each other, which wouldn't lead to conception."

"I know there are, but I also know myself. Once I start…feeling pleasure, I mean…I won't want to stop."

You beautiful, wondrous dream maiden. "Is that so?"

She nodded. Then her furrowed brow relaxed, and she gave him a seductive smile. "But I could enjoy *you.*"

His manhood twitched at the prospect. If he gave her the reins, what would she do? He *had* to know. "Then I am yours to enjoy."

Her smile grew. "Prithee remove your belt."

His pulse raced as he obeyed.

"And your tunic," she continued, pointing. "In fact, doff all of your clothes."

"Even my breeches?"

"Especially those."

He couldn't disrobe fast enough. When the last stitch of clothing hit the ground, her gaze scorched a path all the way down to his feet and back up again.

"You…are…incredible," she breathed. Stooping, she grabbed his tunic and spread it out on the grass.

"Lie down."

He did as she asked, and she knelt beside him. Leaning over, she kissed him full on the mouth. When he would've deepened the kiss, she pulled away and moved her lips to his right ear. Her breath hot on his skin, she bit his earlobe.

He shivered, then closed his eyes and smiled. She was full of surprises.

"God, Hugh." Her lips, breath, and musical voice tickled his ear. "You have no idea how wet I am."

His eyes shot open. Never had he wanted a woman more. He slid his hand along her thigh.

She covered his hand with hers and pushed it away. "Oh no you don't. This is all about you."

Raking her fingers through his chest hair, she bent over him and closed her mouth around his right nipple. Pleasure streamed through him as she licked and bit first that nipple and then the other. She kissed his ribs, his belly, his hips.

She paused just above that part of him which craved her most. He held his breath.

Lifting her head, she straightened. "I have an idea." She pulled her long braid over her shoulder, untied it, and with deft fingers, loosened the plait until her golden hair hung wavy and free. Then she leaned over and wrapped silken tendrils around his engorged shaft.

It took a moment, but he found his tongue. "Ardyth…what are you—"

Her hand closed around him, and she stroked him through the soft barrier her hair had created. "How does this feel?"

His heart pounded. "Quite…astonishing."

Suddenly, she loosened her grip and unwrapped

her hair from his sex. "Perhaps just my hand." She caressed him from base to tip, then took a firm hold of him again. "Shall I move it fast?"

Her hot hand demonstrated, and he sucked in his breath. She was a born temptress.

"Or slowly?" Again, she showed him her meaning, then repeated. "Fast? Or slow?"

His heart hammered in his chest, but he found the will to speak. "Am I supposed to answer that?"

She grinned. "Actually, no. I have a better idea." She bent down and with her tongue, encircled the tip of his manhood.

Sweet Mother of—

She released her hold on his shaft to cradle the orbs beneath it. Then she gripped him again and took him into her mouth.

He gasped, then groaned as her mouth and hand worked in unison. The valley…aye, the entire world around them faded into insignificance; all that mattered was the exquisite feel of her around him. Pleasure built within, taking him closer and closer to the brink.

"Ah!" A bolt of bliss shot through him, nearly blinding him. He shuddered as she slowed her ministrations.

With a smile, she released him. "Are you all right?"

He strove to catch his breath. "How…where did you…? Never mind. I don't care."

She giggled. "I thought you might like it."

He pushed himself into a sitting position. "Like? 'Tis far too tame a word." He caressed her cheek. "Thank you, Ardyth."

Her brown eyes glowed brighter than the glittering

water. "You're welcome."

"I only wish you'd allow me to serve *you* thus." He slid his hand down to her shoulder.

Color flooded her cheeks. "Believe me, I wish for that too, but—"

"Why must there be a 'but'? Would a pleasurable interlude truly affect your future?"

"It might." She pulled her hair forward over one shoulder and started to plait it quickly.

Following her cue, he reached for his breeches and started to dress. "You said you have plans…" *Pray, share them with me.*

Her fingers slowed. "I did say that, didn't I?" The same faraway look he'd seen before overtook her features.

He didn't want her far away. He needed her here, beside him. Today, tomorrow, and for as long a time as she would grant him.

Her brow creased. Was she reconsidering her plans? What could he do to make that happen?

His heart quickened its pace, and he grinned. That heart had quite a test this afternoon; his manhood stirred again at the thought of what caused its exertion. But it could stand a little more…tonight.

With haste, he threw on his tunic and crouched to retrieve his belt. "I just remembered something that requires my attention." He fastened his belt and held out his hand to Ardyth. "Come. Let's return to Seacrest."

Her frown deepened as he helped her up. "Are you upset with me?"

He cradled her face in his hands and gave her a brief but heartfelt kiss. "I've never been more pleased with anyone in my life."

Her answering smile was a glory to behold.

Reluctantly, he released her. Another grin spread across his face as he snatched his stockings from the grass and reached for his boots. She might have plans, but he had a few of his own.

Chapter Fourteen

That night after supper, Ardyth entertained the hall with one song, then went right into a story. It was a mystery she'd plotted that afternoon, after she and Hugh returned from the outing that left her desperate to distract herself from her swelling emotions and hornier-than-hell body.

To judge from her audience's spellbound expressions, this story was one of her best. Even Isobel seemed riveted. She sat between Hugh and Lillian, both of whom had come down from the gallery to enjoy the evening's diversion side by side with the people for the first time. Wide-eyed and on the edge of his seat, Corbin clung to his mother's arm. Giles and Archdeacon Dominy sat together, listening with rapt attention for the most part, but trading occasional glances nonetheless. Close by sat Bertram, and beside him, Ranulf cozied up to Juliana.

After the final applause, Ranulf whispered in Juliana's ear. Then on swift feet, he approached Dominy and steered him away from Giles. No doubt he was trying to ingratiate himself with the archdeacon for Juliana's sake. Giles didn't suffer long for company, though; Bertram joined him five seconds later, perhaps intent on soothing the minstrel's sore ego after the ban of his beloved treasure songs.

Ardyth's gaze inevitably sought Hugh. A short

manservant rushed up to him and imparted news of some sort. Hugh gave him a nod followed by a brief reply, and the man scuttled away.

Her pulse quickened as Hugh started toward her, with Lillian and Isobel in tow. A strand of his jet-black hair fell toward his right eye, and her fingers itched to coax it back into place.

"A wonderful story," said Lillian. Her lovely gray eyes were so like her son's.

"Thank you. I'm happy you approve."

"Oh, I do. The ending, in particular, was delightful."

"Stirring indeed," Hugh intoned with his velvety voice. "Lady Ardyth, may I steal you away for a moment?"

Before she could answer, Isobel moved to stand between them. "My lord, I hoped the three of us—Lady Seacrest, you and I—might take a turn in the garden."

Lillian stepped in. "A lovely idea, Lady Isobel, but I was about to ask you to join me in the chapel."

Isobel's face fell. "The chapel? Wherefore?"

"'Tis time we embroidered a new altar cloth for Father Jacques. I'd like you to come with me so we might study the space and determine the best colors and design."

"Cannot we do so on the morrow?"

Lillian smiled sweetly. "I think not. Let's go thither now."

Isobel looked to Lord Seacrest but found no help from that quarter. With a sigh, she followed Lillian out of the hall.

Ardyth met Hugh's gaze. "You said you wanted to steal me away?"

"Aye, and for more than a moment."

"May I ask why?"

"Tonight is all about pleasure. Yours."

Her jaw dropped, then she swallowed hard. "What do you mean?"

His grin had a roguish slant to it. "Come with me."

Her heart and stomach aflutter, she walked with him all the way to the spiral stairs which led to his bedchamber. She paused and arched an eyebrow. "Your chamber?"

He nodded in silence. "Where else?"

"Hugh, I—"

"Shh." He placed a finger at her lips, and she was tempted to bite it. "Do you trust me?"

"More than I trust myself at the moment."

He chuckled and motioned to the stairs. "After you."

Her legs felt wobbly as she climbed the stone steps, but she made it to the top. She crossed the threshold and halted just inside. "I don't believe it!"

A round, wooden, cloth-lined tub stood before the fireplace, which teemed with dancing flames. She stepped closer, and her eyes widened at the sight of rose petals—red, white, and pink—floating on the surface of the water. The bath board held various-sized cloths and a small ceramic container, which she assumed contained soft soap similar to the kind she used in her daily ablutions.

Thud. Swoosh. Clunk.

She turned. Hugh stood before the closed and bolted door.

His smoldering gaze held hers. "That day in the solar, the first time you wrote for me, you expressed a desire for a bath."

"I remember."

"I myself bathed earlier, and all the while, I thought of you. I knew I must give you the same pleasure…here in my chamber, where you can enjoy some privacy." He motioned toward the tub. "Please."

She almost swooned. A hot bath! All to herself. It had been so long since she felt really clean. "You don't have to ask me twice!"

In a burst of movement, she pulled off her overtunic. Her inner tunic followed, and then her slippers and stockings. All that remained was her smock.

Hugh's gaze locked onto the thin garment. "Aren't you going to doff your chemise?"

"In a moment. I assume you have a straight razor."

"I have. Why do you ask?"

She removed her leather hair tie and started to unravel the braid. "May I borrow it?"

"Wherefore?"

"I want to shave the hair from my legs and armpits." Since arriving in the twelfth century, she'd enjoyed her reprieve from shaving, but she couldn't pass up this chance.

He gave her a sidewise look. "Why?"

Because I'm feeling skanky. "Does it matter why? Pray, let me use it."

With a shrug, he crossed the room to a small table and grabbed the instrument. Then he set it on the bath board. "There you are. Shall I close the window?"

"'Tis warm in here. Let's leave it open."

He gave her a nod and folded his arms. "So…your chemise?"

"I'll doff it as soon as you look away."

He cocked an eyebrow. "In sooth? After what we shared this afternoon?"

She blushed at the memory. Never had she been so bold with a man. She'd only slept with two anyway: the first, a one-night stand to whom she lost her virginity, not because she particularly liked the guy, but because she wanted to experience what all her female friends already had; the second, "Judas John" in what she thought was a committed relationship, until he proved his true aim was to steal her research.

She had *never* needed a man. But now with Hugh, she found herself longing for what her parents had: true and lasting love. She loved him; of that she was positive. Yet even if he returned her feelings, how could their love last? Meg from Ravenwood had stated clearly that she was destined—one might say doomed—to return to the future. She couldn't play Ardyth in Wonderland forever.

"You *do* recall this afternoon, don't you?" Hugh prompted, unfolding his arms.

She forced herself to smile, embracing the here and now. "How could I forget? But if you see me nude, there's a good chance you'll want to touch me—which I'll want too. And once that happens, it's a slippery slope to…"

"What?"

Paradise. "You know perfectly well what." She pointed to the cushioned, low-backed chair before the fire. "Sit there like a good little boy and keep your eyes on the fire."

He laughed, then with a pointed look, advanced toward her. "Need I remind you I'm a grown man?"

Her heart flip-flopped. "Trust me, I need no reminder. And yet I repeat: sit."

He hesitated only a moment, then heaved a long sigh. "Very well." He strode toward the hearth.

Once he was seated, she set her hair tie on the bath board, pulled off her chemise, and stepped into the warm, rose-scented water. With a sigh of sheer delight, she sat down—facing both the fire and his back to keep an eye on him—and began to bathe. The soap smelled of lavender, and she worked a good amount of it into her hair. After rinsing, she checked to make sure Hugh's back was still turned, then looked up at the stag tapestry.

"Is that stag meant to represent *you*, standing proud and virile, yet alone amidst a sea of trees?" Her gaze found the bed with its linen sheets and deep red curtains.

"How colorfully you put it. To answer your question, no. But it has always been one of my favorite hangings, and I wanted it here."

"And what you want, you get." A slight pause followed, and she tore her gaze from the bed and continued to wash.

"Most of the time," he said at last. There was a catch in his voice. What was he thinking?

She frowned at the tapestry. He shouldn't be alone. He deserved a lifetime of love. Children. Everything she wanted to give him but couldn't. If only they'd met in *her* time.

Henri leapt to mind. He was definitely Hugh's doppelganger, but the surface level meant nothing. The heart and mind, the *soul*, that's what mattered. In all the world, across every era, there was one Hugh. Just one.

"And you, Ardyth. Do you always get what you want?"

"Not always. Sometimes." Water splashed as she stood.

"Are you finished bathing?"

"No. I'm standing so I can shave my legs." *Carefully!* She grabbed the razor and focused on the task.

Another, longer pause. "The Church sees the stag as the enemy of snakes."

"Even if that stag has a 'snake' of his own?"

"By snake, do you mean his member?"

"I do indeed."

"Are we talking about man or animal?"

"Both, I imagine."

He chortled. "Your mind is a marvel."

"Thank you, my lord." She finished shaving her legs, miraculously without drawing blood. Sinking down into the water, which felt cooler now, she started on an armpit.

"My lord? Why so formal?"

"No reason…Hugh."

"That's better." He lifted his arms and pulled his tunic over his head.

She frowned. "Why are you undressing?"

"'Tis hot."

It certainly is! She drank in the sight of his bare back and the writhing flames which seemed to reach for him, as she longed to do. Then she shook her head, replaced the razor on the bath board, and stood once more. Seizing a large drying cloth, she stepped out of the tub onto the rush-covered floor.

"*Now* are you done?" He still faced the fire.

"My, aren't we impatient? I'm drying off."

"Good. I'm turning around."

Wait! She managed to cover her torso before his gaze reached her.

He gave her a little smile. "All wrapped up."

"Well, close enough." She ogled his bare chest, then forced her gaze back up to his face.

His smile dissolved as his expression turned serious. "I must see the results of your shaving." With powerful strides, he closed the gap between them.

She swallowed hard. "If you must…" Holding the edge of the cloth in place with one hand, she lifted the other arm.

Lightly, he touched her armpit. "Curious." Squatting, he ran his fingertips from her ankle up to her knee. "So soft and smooth."

"I think you'd better—"

"The time for thinking is past." In a rush, he stood and swooped her up in his arms.

She gasped. "What are you doing?"

"The only thing I *can* do." He strode to the bed and laid her on it.

"What in—"

"Lie still." He crouched beside the bed, then straightened again, stretched out one of her arms, and tied her wrist to the bedstead with a ribbon.

"Hugh…"

"Trust me." He kissed her neck, and she shivered. Quickly, he tied her other wrist to the opposite side of the bed. "Do you promise not to kick me? Or shall I tie your feet?"

"I shan't promise anything until you explain yourself."

He joined her atop the bed and sat on his heels. "'Tis very simple. I am in your debt for the pleasure you gave me, and I always settle my debts."

Her pulse raced. "This isn't a good idea."

"You're right. 'Tis a *great* idea, and I must repay you."

"I don't need payment." It was a lie. Her whole body felt heavy with need and ached for his touch.

"Perhaps not, but *I* need it. Rest assured, I shan't force you in any way, so you needn't fear pregnancy."

"Damn it, Hugh!"

"Curse me if you will, but know this: I intend to pleasure you, and if this be the only way, then by God's blood, so shall it be."

Slowly, as though unwrapping a fragile gift, he opened the drying cloth. He sucked in his breath. "Ardyth…you are beauty made flesh."

He did have a way with words, though she could think of none that formed a lucid response. But maybe she didn't have to respond. Maybe the best course of action was to lie back and surrender to this remarkable medieval man. His very gaze worshipped her. In all her life, she'd never felt so feminine, so revered.

Gently, he squeezed her breasts, then leaned forward to flick his tongue over first one nipple and then the other. He lavished attention on each breast, caressing, sucking, savoring her curves until her nipples were rock hard and she was damp between the legs.

He kissed his way down her belly and blew on the hair she *hadn't* shaved. He inhaled deeply, then moaned. "Your scent is divine. I must have a proper taste."

His tongue explored her moist folds, tracing and

teasing until he plunged it inside her. She gasped and wiggled beneath the pleasurable onslaught.

"Sweet nectar," he breathed, lifting his mouth toward a higher target. His tongue found her clit and claimed it.

God, yes! She arched her back, then lifted her hips. "Aye, Hugh. Oh, aye…"

His expert tongue moved slowly, tenderly. Her passion built with each and every stroke.

She wanted to grab his hair, but her hands were tied. "A little faster. That's it. Aye!"

He was a god. Perfect and persistent. Pushing her to the brink and then…

She cried out as her pleasure exploded, sending shock waves of sensation through her entire body. When she came back to earth, she opened her eyes and licked her lips. "Hugh?"

He lifted his head and grinned up at her. "Ardyth?"

His expression was a mixture of satisfaction and yearning. He wanted her, and God help her, she wanted him. What were the odds she'd get pregnant from just one time?

She'd cross that bridge *if* she came to it. All that mattered was now. One precious night with the man she loved, creating a memory she'd cherish all her life in whatever cold, distant future awaited her.

She took a deep breath. "I…I've changed my mind."

****

Basking in her glorious scent, Hugh gazed up at her. Sweat glistened on her face, and in her eyes, he read passion and resolve.

His heart beat faster, and he hardly dared ask.

"About what?"

"I warned you if we started, I wouldn't stop, and I was right. I want you, Hugh. Completely."

His manhood throbbed as he sat up. An overpowering need seized his body, mind, and soul, shaking him to the core. He *had* to be with her, to bind their two selves into one.

"Are you sure?" He ran a hand over her silken thigh.

"Never more so." Her brown eyes glowed, but she gave him a sheepish grin. "If you'd be so kind as to untie me…"

"Of course." He made quick work of it and threw the ribbons on the floor. Then he lay over her and kissed her with all the desire surging through his being. He thrust his tongue into her mouth, as he had her feminine channel. In a few moments, his desperate member would find a home in that wet, perfumed heaven.

Her hands clasped his buttocks. She bit his lip, and he groaned in response.

She lifted a hand to his mouth. "Did I hurt you?"

"No! My wild, sweet owl." He tongued her left ear and bit the lobe.

She shivered beneath him. "Hugh, do you remember that day by the sea…when I told you I'd never ridden aside?"

He raised his head to gaze into her shining eyes. "You said when you ride something, you spread your legs."

"That's right. May I now ride *you*?"

His manhood leapt in response. "You may." He rolled onto his back, pulling her with him.

She straddled him and gripped his shaft. Slowly, she welcomed every inch of it into her tight, hot sheath. The pleasure was acute…and then she started to move.

Christ's fingernails!

She moved deliberately, without haste, as if to cherish each sensation. Her musical moans surrounded them both in a web of enchanted bliss. Soon she rode faster, then frantically, until she screamed her satisfaction.

Her silken folds squeezed him again and again in spasms of ecstasy. He gritted his teeth, determined to hold back his release until she'd reached another summit.

Her movements slowed. "Your turn, Hugh."

He shook his head. "Not until you peak again."

"You're joking."

He stared into her soulful eyes. "No, Ardyth. *After you.*" Holding her gaze, he sought her pleasure spot and pushed with his thumb.

"Oh! Well, if you insist…" She began her ride anew, and he continued to thrum the bud of her desire. "Don't stop, Hugh. You wonderful…marvelous man."

She rode him faster, wilder. His heart thumped in his chest, and he squeezed his eyes shut, conjuring any image which would keep him from spilling his seed too soon.

Crop yields. Dancing dogs. A puppet show.

Ardyth cried out again, and he opened his eyes. The look on her face might denote pain or piercing pleasure, but he knew 'twas the latter. Now he could let go and allow her tremors to take him home.

He clutched her thighs and surrendered all to her magic. He flew higher and higher, soaring beyond time and tempests to the pinnacle of pleasure that awaited him. With a growl, he bucked his hips on a burst of soul-shattering bliss.

The next thing he knew, Ardyth moved off of him and the bed and scurried toward the tub. He turned his head to follow her retreat. "Where are you—"

"Just washing myself. Don't fret. But now that I think of it, I should probably go back to my own bed."

His heart twisted. "I don't want you to go."

"I cannot stay all night. What would your mother think? Or Lady Isobel?"

He frowned. She was right. "Then stay for just a little while, if only to rest your body." That body was flushed from their lovemaking and the closest thing to perfection he'd ever beheld.

"Well...all right." She threw the washcloth into the tub and hurried back into bed.

She turned on her side, facing the fire, and he gathered her into his arms from behind. He inhaled her scent and kissed her shoulder.

She sighed. "What are you thinking?"

The fleshy curve of her backside threatened to arouse him again, but he would let her rest. "That I would stop time and stay in this moment as long as possible. And you?"

"The very same."

"Hmm...imagine that." The rhythm of her breathing and the crackling fire lulled him into a deep, contented sleep.

Chapter Fifteen

A rich, low sigh woke Ardyth. Serenity enveloped her, as did Hugh's arms and manly scent. His breaths were deep and even; he must've moaned in his sleep. Soft light filtered into the room through the open window.

Good. The dead of night hadn't arrived yet, so she had time to do the "walk of shame" back to her tiny chamber before anyone missed her.

Yet shame refused her summons. It felt so right to lie in his arms…for two more seconds before she snuck out of bed. Nature called, emphatically.

With care and as little sound as possible, she pushed his right arm off her body and slipped out of bed. She grabbed the chamber pot from under the bed and relieved herself, then stood and patted the hair on her head. Mostly dry but tangled, for there'd been no time for grooming after the bath.

She strode to the table where Hugh had kept his razor and spied a comb. Quickly, she worked the tats out of her hair, then braided it, and crossed to the tub. She grabbed her hair tie from the bath board and secured her plait.

All at once, she noticed the hearth. *Holy shit! I'm screwed!*

The fire had completely burnt out. They'd slept for hours, and it was early morning light streaming through the window.

Hugh slumbered on, and it was just as well. Let him dream in peace. It was *her* reputation on the line, not his. She had to throw on her clothes and haul ass back to her room. Pronto!

Minutes later, she stole through the snores and whimpers in the great hall toward her room. Flickering light from within spilled out into a small portion of the hall.

Damn! At least one of the sisters was awake and had lit the oil lamp. With a roll of her eyes, she braced herself and entered the chamber.

Isobel! Of course. She sat alone on her mattress and wore one of her best scowls. "Where have you been?" she asked in a low voice.

"It matters not. Where's Juliana?"

She crossed her arms. "*Lady* Juliana was talking with Ranulf in the hall yesternight when last I saw her. She's been gone all night…as have you. My uncle will be interested to learn of this latest transgression."

"Whose? Mine or your sister's?"

"Why, you impudent—"

"Lower your voice! Almost everyone is still abed, and you'd do well to think of someone other than yourself for a change."

"What about you? Have you been thinking of someone else? Or perhaps *serving* them in some capacity?"

Are you calling me a whore? Ardyth's eyes narrowed. "Be careful. There may come a day when you regret your words."

"Are you threatening me?"

"I'm reminding you that words are weapons. Some

172

wounds, once inflicted, can never be healed."

"Hmph. By the way, someone left you a message." She pointed to a bit of folded parchment on the smaller mattress.

"Any idea who?"

Isobel shrugged. "I didn't read it, but 'twas there when I came to bed. Not that I slept at all."

Ardyth picked up the parchment and read silently: *"I have Lady Seacrest. Tell no one and meet us in the sea cave. Come alone or she dies."*

Her stomach lurched. "Oh no," she said in Modern English.

"What is it?" Isobel demanded.

"Did you and Lady Seacrest leave the chapel together last night?"

She knitted her brow. "No. She wanted to stay longer, so I left her there. Why?"

Ignoring the question, Ardyth examined the note. The flourish on the "t"s was distinctive; it resembled the script on the message *she'd* been purported to write. Clearly, both were penned by the same person: the mastermind behind Hugh's assault. And now he'd kidnapped Lillian!

Avoiding Isobel's gaze, Ardyth shoved the parchment into her slipper for safe keeping. "It doesn't concern you." She straightened and bolted out of the room.

Medieval ladies weren't supposed to run, but thankfully, everyone in sight was still asleep. She hightailed it to solar, grabbing a wall torch along the way, and darted behind the unicorn screen.

Lifting the trapdoor, she paused. *Should I wake Hugh?*

No. She couldn't risk Lillian's life, and there wasn't time. The message sat waiting on her bed all night, while God-knew-what happened to Hugh's mother. Had she been beaten? Tortured? All for some stupid treasure that didn't exist?

She started down the stairs, pulled the door closed over her head, and descended to the cold, dank tunnel. Grateful for the torch gripped in her hand, she scurried through the darkness, pondering the burning questions that needed answers.

Who had sent the note? *A man, most likely, and an educated one.*

Did he think Lillian would reveal the location of the fictional treasure? *Maybe, and if he struck out with her as he did with Hugh, he must think I know something.*

When and where did he kidnap her? *Probably not from her room. From the chapel? Isobel said she left her alone, but could she have been in on it?*

The trouble started when Archdeacon Dominy arrived. Could he be the architect behind it all? *He's educated: check. From York: double check. A total scumbag: check to the tenth power!* Still, he was a man of God. In theory, at least. If he cared about his immortal soul, would he stoop so low?

She reached the end of the tunnel and sniffed the air. It smelled earthy and new. Rain had come in the night, and the cliff walk was muddy. If only she'd worn her boots!

Seeing no holder for the torch, she plunged it into the mire where it stuck, its flames defeated. Then she schlepped along the path to the sea cave, hesitating just before the entrance.

Hopefully, the creep was alone. But how fit was he? If by some miracle she managed to knock him out, she'd need something to tie him up.

Stockings. She sat on a wet rock and removed her shoes and hose.

A sudden gust whipped her. It blew the parchment out of her slipper and over the edge of the cliff.

Damn! The tide was coming in, and the wind would carry the note right down to the water. So much for that clue!

With a sigh, she replaced her shoes and stood. Slippers clutched in her hand, she peeked into the cave.

Apart from the sound of encroaching seawater, the hollow was empty.

She frowned. Were they in one of the three tunnels?

She dashed inside and down the ledge, all the way to the bottom. Listening intently for any sound other than the ocean, she explored each tunnel for about a minute. She had no desire to get lost, so that was as long as she dared.

No Lillian. No bad guy.

Was it a lie? A ploy to lure her down here? Maybe the intent was to press *her* for information, not Lillian, who was likely safe in her bed.

So where was the bastard? Did he get tired of waiting and leave?

The water sloshed on, reverberating off the walls of the cave. Mesmeric, but unhelpful.

What the actual hell? Her frown deepened as she trudged up the ledge, out of the cave, and back to the Rock Man.

The cries of gulls pecked the morning air. An

unusual number of them soared near the cliff. From the sound of it, they crowded the shore below.

Curious, she peered over the edge. *Oh my God!*

A man in white lay prostrate on the sand. His head was twisted at a weird angle. Even from a distance, his face and hands looked purple.

There was no doubt. Archdeacon Dominy was dead.

****

Hugh woke with a start. Ashen-faced, Ardyth rushed to the bedside. She was dressed in her clothes from the night before, but her slippers and the hem of her gown were caked with mud.

"Hugh, you must dress and come immediately." Stress threaded her voice.

He sat bolt upright. "What is amiss?"

"Archdeacon Dominy. He's dead!"

His jaw dropped. "How do you know?"

"I just saw his body. On the beach."

He leapt out of bed and reached for the chamber pot. "Has anyone else seen it?"

"I don't think so. 'Tis early yet. Shall I look away while you…"

He gave her a wry look. "Why hide what has already been seen?"

"True."

After relieving himself, he turned to her. Her brow was creased, and she fidgeted. He'd never seen her so nervous. On impulse, he pulled her close and gave her a quick kiss on the lips. "If only there were time…"

"I know, but there isn't. You must hurry."

He released her and hastened to dress. "Where on the beach is he?"

"On the side with all the boats. He must've fallen from quite a height."

"The battlements?"

She shook her head. "The guards would've seen or heard him. My guess is, he fell from the cliff. He's lying right beneath the Rock Man."

He encircled his tunic with a belt, and as he fastened it, her words hit home. "But that would mean…"

"He used the secret passage."

Frowning, he shoved his foot into a boot. "Perhaps he *was* behind the plot against me. 'Twould make sense for him to use the passage toward that end, but…how could he have known about it?"

She bit her lip. "Could Bertram have—"

"Impossible." He pulled on his other boot. "I've known Bertram all my life. He would never betray our trust. Come. Take me to the archdeacon before all of Seacrest awakens."

They flew down the stairs but slowed their pace in the hall. There were a few murmurs and stirrings. It wouldn't be long before everyone was up and about.

"My lord!" The harsh whisper stopped them.

'Twas Isobel, bustling toward him. His stomach churned. She wouldn't take the news of her uncle's death well.

"Whither are you two going?"

"I'll explain later."

She stomped her foot, and a maidservant on the floor nearby flinched in her sleep. "I won't be cast aside."

He took a deep breath and blew it out in a rush. "Then keep quiet and come with us."

They exited the hall and keep and continued through the upper bailey garden to the gatehouse.

The gatekeeper ran a hand through his ruffled, auburn hair. "My lord," he rasped.

"Philippe."

They hurried down to the beach. The wind blew in gusts, attacking his face and clothes in sudden bursts of fury.

His chest tightened as he turned to Isobel. "You must prepare yourself."

"For what, pray?"

They veered right. The gulls were loud, excited. The next instant, they halted in front of the cause.

Archdeacon Dominy, glassy-eyed and discolored. His bruised head lay at an impossible angle, and dark blood stained the sand near his mouth.

Isobel shrieked and threw herself against him. He wrapped a comforting arm around her trembling frame.

After a long moment, she raised her head and sought his gaze. "What happened?"

"We don't know," he said gently.

"We?"

"Lady Ardyth and I."

She pulled away and aimed a dagger-sharp stare at her rival. "What has *she* to do with it?"

Ardyth took a step toward her. "I discovered him and ran to fetch Hugh."

"*Lord Seacrest*, you mean."

"Right. Lord Seacrest. I think he fell from up there." She pointed toward the cliff, then met Hugh's gaze. "Or was pushed."

He raised his eyebrows. *Pushed. Murdered?*

Isobel pointed an imperious finger at her. "*You* did

it!"

Her eyes wide, Ardyth backed away. "What?"

"How else would you know where to find the body? You were out all night and had plenty of time to do it."

He stepped between them. "She was with me last night."

Isobel's mouth opened and closed. Then her blue eyes narrowed. "*All* night?"

Come to think of it, he had no idea how long she stayed in his chamber. "Much of it." He turned to Ardyth. "When did you leave?"

She shrugged. "I don't know exactly. Around first light. But look!" She motioned to the corpse, which more and more gulls came to investigate. "'Tis obvious he's been here a while because…"

"Has he?" Isobel interrupted in a haughty tone. "It seems you know a lot about dead bodies. How?"

"*Tee-vee*," Ardyth muttered.

"What did you say?"

"Naught. A Saxon word."

"You should speak the Norman tongue in a Norman stronghold. Unless, of course, you have something to hide."

Ardyth clenched her fists at her sides. "I have nothing to hide!"

"You hated my uncle. He told me you threatened him."

"I didn't actually mean it!"

Hugh recalled his conversation with Dominy. He'd defended Ardyth's character by stating that owls were superb hunters of vermin. The archdeacon was like unto a rat. Had she hunted him down? *She's told me again and again not to underestimate her.* Her warning words rushed back to him. *"If he wants to draw breath, he'd better not bother me again."*

Isobel glared at her. "Oh, you meant it. I'm certain." She turned to him. "And a short while ago, in our chamber, she threatened *me*."

"I did not!" Ardyth protested.

"Either Saxon brains have short memories or you're lying. My uncle was right about you. You're evil to the core!"

He placed a firm hand on Isobel's shoulder. "Calm yourself." Dropping his hand, he turned back to Ardyth. "I must ask…what led you to find the archdeacon?"

"I went to the sea cave." Her pointed gaze seemed to indicate she'd done so by way of the secret passage.

"Wherefore?"

"There was a note waiting for me in my chamber." She looked to Isobel. "You were there. You saw it."

He turned to Isobel for answers. Triumph shone in her eyes, and her reply was slow and deliberate. "What note?"

Ardyth's face was a mask of horror. "The message on my bed. The one that—"

"I saw no message." Isobel's voice held strength, calm, and confidence.

Hugh glanced up at the Rock Man. The archdeacon clearly fell from that spot. Until now, no one but his family, Bertram, and Ardyth had walked there. His steward was beyond suspicion, and Ardyth had all but admitted she'd been there earlier.

His stomach knotted as a jumble of images and information converged in his mind. The first time he showed her the sea cave, she asked about the treasure.

180

She had a lot of free time; could she have slipped away to York and hired the men who attacked him? The idea that an owl told her where to find him that dreadful night was illogical. Perhaps she already knew of his dilemma because she'd arranged it. What if the whole incident was an attempt to gain not only treasure, but his trust?

No! He couldn't believe it. And yet…she'd mentioned plans. Did they include thievery and fleeing northward with untold riches?

"There *was* a note," she said now, motioning emphatically with her hands. "Lady Isobel saw it."

Speech abandoned him. Suppositions crowded his mind.

"Hugh! Say something!"

He fought to strike the doubt from his expression, but failed. Her face crumpled. She spun around, lifted her skirts, and dashed off around the rocky headland.

He turned to Isobel. "Return to the keep. Notify my mother and your sister of what has happened."

"What will *you* do?"

"What I must."

He ran after Ardyth along the narrow strip of land that resisted the rising tide. He caught her from behind.

With a shout, she broke free, turning to face him. "Why are you following me? Why don't you run back to Isobel?"

Hot blood coursed in his veins. "Because I seek answers from *you*!"

"She's lying, Hugh."

"Lady Isobel has her faults, but I've never known her to speak falsehoods."

"Well, she's speaking them now!"

He took a deep breath, and released it slowly. "Very well. Where is the note?"

"It blew away when I was up on the cliff."

Convenient. He frowned. "The cliff from which the archdeacon fell?" *Or was pushed.* "What were you doing there?"

"Saving your mother, I thought."

His chest tightened. "My mother?"

She nodded. "The note was written in the same hand as the fake message *you* received. It said, 'I have Lady Seacrest. Tell no one and meet us in the sea cave. Come alone or she dies.'"

"So you went by way of the secret passage."

"I did, but no one was there. On my way back up, I noticed the number of gulls around and looked down. That's when I saw the body."

Her story was sounding less and less plausible, but he wanted to believe her. Suppose the archdeacon made advances toward her. Would she push him over the edge to save herself? But then, why was he on the cliff walk at all? "Are you sure you didn't…" He couldn't finish the question.

Her eyes widened. "What? Send him flying myself?"

"You did assault Degarre."

"To save *you*!"

"Or to gain a treasure?"

She stared into his eyes for what seemed an eternity. Then comprehension and shock rolled in waves across her face. "Holy Mary, Mother of God. You think I'm behind it all."

His mind and heart were at war. "I don't want to think it."

"How could you possibly…you know me!"

"No, I don't. Not really. Who are you, Ardyth?"

She hesitated only a moment, then lifted her chin and stared him straight in the eye. "I'll tell you, if you'll listen."

"I'm listening."

"My name is Ardyth Nightshade, and I *am* Lord Nihtscua's kinswoman…only I'm his descendant. I come from the year nineteen hundred and eighty-six, and I—"

"What?" Incredulity overcame him.

"Let me finish! I'm a university student in history, and I traveled back to this time…unexpectedly, I might add…through a magical site near Nihtscua called Woden's Stair. I'm supposed to travel back to my own time through Woden's Circle at Ravenwood sometime soon, though I don't know when. You can write to Lord and Lady Nihtscua for confirmation of this…or to Meg, that is, Lady Margaret of Ravenwood."

He gaped at her, wrestling with her explanation. How could it be true? It clashed so completely with everything he understood of the world. His heart sank like a weight in water.

Her lovely features contorted with pain. "Hugh, you must believe me!"

Chapter Sixteen

The ocean pounded the shore. Ardyth held her breath and waited for Hugh's answer. Every fiber of her being needed his trust.

Some subtle yet essential element within his steel-gray eyes broke, then retreated. "How can I?"

Oh my God. Not again.

The specter of false accusation—which had haunted her ever since John's betrayal and her department head's response—was back, only one hundred times worse. The man she loved had lost faith in her, and that truth was like a punch in the gut. Never had she felt so alone.

There was nothing for her in the year 1102. Not anymore. Meg had said she'd know when the time came to return to 1986, and it was here, now.

She tore her gaze from his and ran back the way she'd come, up to the gatehouse, past an open-mouthed Philippe, and through the garden. The chapel bells rang the first hour as she dashed up the steps and into the keep. In the hall, where servants yawned, stretched, and rose to start their day, she slowed her pace to a brisk walk.

Before the wooden screen of her chamber, Juliana and Ranulf stood gazing into each other's eyes. She knew that look: the telltale morning-after glow and starry-eyed stare of two lovers who'd just discovered one another. She and Hugh had shared such a look not long ago, before everything got shot to hell. Envy rose within her, but she squashed it with genuine goodwill toward the couple and stopped in front of them. As one, they turned to her.

"Ah, Lady Ardyth," said Ranulf.

Juliana gave Ardyth's arm a gentle pat. "I just spoke with my sister. Are you all right?"

Ardyth raised her eyebrows. "Am *I* all right? Didn't she tell you about your uncle?"

"She did, and I must admit to a strange sense of relief. 'Twas Isobel who liked him, not I. I'm sorry she accused you of killing him. Lady Seacrest is still abed, but once she wakes, I'm certain Isobel will give her an earful."

Great. Just what I need: another Seacrest who'll hate me.

Ranulf shook his head regretfully. "Both of us know you wouldn't do such a thing."

She gave him a sad smile. "Thank you. I would others felt the same."

"Others?" Juliana's eyes widened. "Not his lordship!"

Ardyth nodded. "Which is why I'm leaving Seacrest today…almost this instant, once I pack a few things. If you'll excuse me." She brushed past them, entered the chamber, and knelt before her trunks.

Juliana followed her inside. "You cannot leave!"

Ranulf loomed large in the archway. "No indeed."

"I must." She plucked both of Jocelyn's combs from the smaller chest and deposited them into a leather purse. For the rest of her life, she'd cherish them.

"Why should you?" Ranulf asked. "The

archdeacon's death has nothing to do with you. 'Tis likely connected to the treasure."

"The only treasure that interests me is at Woden's Circle."

"Woden's Circle?"

"A place near Ravenwood, the home of Lord Seacrest's brother. That's where I'm headed."

Juliana shook her head. "Not without an escort. There are many dangers for women traveling alone." She looked to Ranulf.

After a brief hesitation, he nodded. "Her ladyship speaks true. I shall escort you."

Ardyth sat back on her heels. "I cannot allow you to—"

"Nonsense." He waved a hand dismissively. "I consider you a friend."

"As do I," Juliana said with a smile. "If not for you, we might never have found one another." She exchanged a tender glance with Ranulf.

"Heaven forbid!" He clicked his heels together. "Right. I'll see to the horses. Lady Ardyth, meet me at the stables as soon as you can." He regarded Juliana. "'Twould hurry us along if you brought food and flask from the kitchens."

She bobbed her head. "At once."

Despite her aching heart, Ardyth summoned a smile. "I'm grateful to you both. But please, tell no one what we're about."

If Hugh got wind of her plans, he'd try to stop her. He might even throw her in the dungeon with the other criminals. *That's where I draw the line!* In fact, she'd already drawn it, the moment she vowed to leave.

****

"Ridiculous!" Lady Seacrest pushed back her shoulders in a show of stubborn resolve Hugh knew all too well. The solar walls rang with the force of her declaration. "Someone *may* have murdered the archdeacon, but that someone was *not* Lady Ardyth."

He began to pace in front of the soulless hearth. "She *did* threaten him."

"Can you blame her? For two pennies, I would've killed the man myself."

"Mother! You don't mean that."

"How right you are. My threat had no substance. Neither had Ardyth's."

He halted. "You use her name informally."

She flashed him a knowing grin. "As do you."

Drained by doubt and an entire morning spent dealing with the archdeacon's demise, he released a long sigh. "I want to trust her." *You've no idea how much.*

"Then do."

"But Lady Isobel—"

"Can go home to her mother. I told her as much when she came to me earlier, casting aspersions on the woman she resents above all others."

"I know she's jealous of Ardyth, but—"

"But nothing. Open your eyes, Son. Have you forgotten how Ardyth saved you from those devils in the dungeon?"

He frowned. "What if she planned the events of that night, just so she could play the hero, like in one of her stories."

She gave him a pointed look. "If you'd seen her face when we learned you were in trouble, you'd know she would *never* hurt you."

"Not even for a fabled treasure?"

Her gray eyes filled with compassion. "Hugh, unless I'm gravely mistaken, *you* are her treasure."

His stomach dropped, and he swallowed hard as he glanced at Ardyth's writing desk. A quill pen waited patiently for her steady, graceful hand. 'Twas not the one he'd made her, though. Where was it? Had she destroyed it in anger? He wouldn't blame her one bit if she had.

He remembered her surprise when he presented the gift. The gratitude in her voice. The tears in her eyes.

Tears brimmed those same eyes today. When he failed to believe in her.

His heart contorted. "Forgive me." Turning away, he strode from the solar to the nearest tower. He climbed the stairs two at a time, up to the battlements and the fresh air he craved. Gray clouds raced overhead as he approached the parapet. Hands on stone, he stared out at the restless sea.

"Ardyth," he whispered.

Warm memories flooded his mind. The first time she plunged into the waves to prove her swimming skills. The magical moment he first heard her sing. The light in her eyes when she told a story, listened to his family history, or challenged his views. The day she insisted they work on the beach and taught him to ride the waves. Her perfect grasp of his childhood loneliness. The way she took charge of his pleasure in the valley yesterday.

Was it only yesterday? So much had happened since.

He loved her humor and intellect. Her touch. Her scent. Her spirit.

She was everything for which he'd longed all these years. Yet, until he met her—nay, until this moment—he hadn't known he wanted it. She answered each question in his life before he even asked it.

His mother was right. She wasn't behind his attack, or the archdeacon's death. She couldn't be.

But had she, in sooth, traveled through time? It might explain her odd behavior on occasion and her unusual talents. But was such a thing possible?

"Talk to me, Hugh." His mother was at his side.

He turned to her. "When I think of taking a wife, of endowing another with the title 'Lady Seacrest,' I cannot imagine anyone but Ardyth."

Lillian's veil billowed in the wind, and her radiant smile waged war on the gloomy day. "My dear, beloved son, I've waited forever to hear you say that. I guess Robert was correct."

"About what?"

"You recall he whispered in my ear the first day of his visit?"

He nodded. "You're finally going to tell me what he said?"

"I am. He gave me a brief message from Lady Margaret of Ravenwood."

"The one they call Meg?" The one to whom Ardyth referred him for proof of her supposed time travel.

"Aye. She said if I ever wanted my eldest to marry, Ardyth was my best chance."

"It seems she was right. I must meet this Meg." *And I must find Ardyth to tell her how I feel.* The midday meal was close at hand. He was bound to see her then.

His mother's gaze slipped to the right, toward

something in the background. Her brow furrowed. "Lady Juliana, staring northward as if…" Her gaze shifted again. "And hither comes Giles."

She started toward them. Curious, he followed.

Juliana turned from the crenellated wall to face Giles, and they conversed. As Hugh and his mother came within hearing distance, Juliana said, "I know nothing about it, Giles. Truly. I have more pressing concerns."

"Oh?" Lillian placed a hand on the lady's arm. "Has your sister told you you're leaving Seacrest?"

Creases streaked Juliana's brow. "She has, but my lady, I would stay longer. At least until…"

"Until what?"

Juliana pressed fingers to her mouth. "I'm not supposed to say."

Hugh frowned. "Perhaps you'd better."

She looked from him to his mother, then to Giles and back again. With a sigh, she nodded. "I'm no good at keeping secrets anyway. I would stay until Ranulf returns. He's escorting Lady Ardyth to Ravenwood."

Heat coursed the length of Hugh's body. "Ravenwood? With Ranulf?"

"We thought it prudent she not travel alone."

Lillian dropped her hand. "We?"

Juliana beamed at her. "Aye. Ranulf and I are to wed."

Hugh relaxed a little. "But why Ravenwood?"

The bride-to-be shrugged. "She said something about Woden's Circle."

Suddenly, Ardyth's words came back to him. *"I'm supposed to travel back to my own time through Woden's Circle."*

Alarm gripped his heart. What if 'twere true? What if he lost her?

He wouldn't! After all this time, he knew what he wanted, *whom* he wanted. He'd be damned if he'd let her go!

"When did they leave?"

"Hours ago."

"My lord." 'Twas Giles. "I must speak with you."

"There's no time, Giles."

"It concerns Lady Ardyth."

Impatience strummed Hugh's nerves. "Aye, I know. You don't trust her."

"No, my lord. I've changed my mind about that."

"I'm glad to hear it, but right now—"

"Forgive me, my lord, but if her ladyship left with Ranulf, you *must* listen!"

Hugh exchanged glances with his mother. For more than three decades, the minstrel had been a fixture at Seacrest. Never had he spoken with such passion. "Very well, Giles. Say what you must."

"Ranulf is always asking about my songs, about the treasure. Then last night, after Lady Ardyth's story…" He regarded Juliana. "…and after he spoke with you…" He turned back to Hugh. "…he pulled Archdeacon Dominy aside. They talked in murmurs for a bit. Then Ranulf left the archdeacon alone in the hall for a time. When he returned, he looked around, all suspicious-like, and went into the ladies' chamber…"

"He did not!" Juliana glared at him.

"I beg your pardon, my lady, but he did. That's why I came hither to ask you about it…thinking you might know why he was there. He had a piece of parchment in his hand when he entered but not when he came out again."

Hugh's pulse quickened. Parchment. The note! Ardyth *had* told the truth about it!

Giles continued. "He whispered again to the archdeacon and led him from the hall. I had a bad feeling about it, so I followed them to your solar."

Lillian looked to Hugh. "The solar?"

His eyes widened. *The secret passage!* He regarded the minstrel. "What did you then, Giles?"

"None of us should've been there. I was uncomfortable, so I left. I ran into Bertram on my way back to the hall and almost told him about it, but I didn't." Again, he regarded Juliana. "Mayhap if I'd spoken up then, your uncle might still be alive."

Her face paled. "But…Ranulf was with *me* last night."

Giles shrugged. "Not then, he wasn't."

Shaking her head, she leaned back against the stone wall. "When Lady Ardyth finished her story, Ranulf told me he had a plan to gain my uncle's favor. He asked me to wait for him in the wool barn…said he'd meet me there anon. I waited so long, I fell asleep. But then he did join me and…and…" She burst into tears.

Lillian put an arm around her. "There, there." Then a look of horror ran through her face as she turned to her son. "Hugh…that means Ardyth…"

"Is on the road with a murderer," Giles finished. "He might harm her."

Hugh's hands clenched into fists, and the wind's wrath fed his will. "By God's bones, I'll kill him first!"

Chapter Seventeen

Twilight spilled over the land and walls of Ravenwood Keep. Ardyth sighed with relief as she and Ranulf slowed their mounts. They'd traveled almost nonstop for two days, pausing only to sleep for the few hours of darkness the summer night afforded.

Ranulf did his best to make conversation during the trip, remarking on their surroundings and praising Juliana to the skies, but Ardyth hadn't felt particularly talkative. Half the time, it seemed her heart was lodged in her throat, and she fought hard to suppress the tears that threatened to escape every time her thoughts swerved toward her last, blissful night with Hugh. Ranulf guessed her feelings for him, and she shared a few details of their relationship. But the wound was too raw, the betrayal too recent, for her to elaborate. Again and again, he prodded her with questions about Woden's Circle, but most she couldn't answer. All she knew was she had to get there ASAP.

Now they'd finally reached Ravenwood, and deliverance was at hand. For a split second, she considered heading on alone and sending her escort back to Seacrest. No need to shock him with things beyond his ken. But images of Degarre and the other thug whose name she never learned, together with the memory of Dominy's purpling corpse, intruded on her thoughts. Better safe than sorry.

She cued her horse to turn right and glanced at Ranulf. "This way."

They rode through the meadow and up a low hill to the impressive stone monument she'd seen as a child when her family toured Ravenwood's ruins. If someone had told her then that one day, she'd see Ravenwood, Druid's Head, and Nihtscua in all their medieval splendor, she'd have thought...

Honestly, she would've smiled and said it didn't surprise her. She believed in magic and miracles, and while she lived at Nightshade Manor, Woden's Stair had an irresistible pull. That same magnetism overcame her the first time she encountered Woden's Circle.

For most of her life, she'd felt out of touch with the modern world, as if some kernel of intuition *knew* she belonged in a different time and place. But now she'd made that journey and found only heartache, a burgeoning dream which could never be fulfilled.

The stones still beckoned. With the way things were, they surely called her back to her *real* home.

Deep in thought, she dismounted. Leaving Ranulf to tie up the horses, she entered the site. The scent of pine needles wafted toward her from the forest that fringed most of the circle. The nine sentinels of stone were twice her height. Three more—two pillars and a capstone—gave the impression of a doorway.

A gateway. The way home!

Rustles sounded within the forest. A handful of ravens appeared and landed on the outer stones. They watched her in silence, as if waiting for the moment she'd sought, yet dreaded.

After a few minutes, Ranulf joined her inside the circle. With a casual air, he stroked one of the stones.

194

"A scenic hiding place."

"I don't intend to hide." Her gaze locked on the stone doorway, and she pursed her lips. *How do I tell you I'm about to travel to the future? If it works, that is.* It had to work!

"Come now, I didn't mean you."

She turned to him. "What *did* you mean?"

"What do you think? The treasure."

She frowned. "I don't understand."

"You said there was treasure at Woden's Circle, and it makes perfect sense. Lord Seacrest moved the loot hither to his brother's estate, didn't he?" His voice had a strange edge to it.

Her skin prickled with warning, and she took a step backward. "There *is* no treasure."

"My father assured me there was. As you know, he and Simon, the first Lord Seacrest, were friends. Why, Simon even showed him the secret passage to the sea cave."

Her stomach lurched. She felt faint, yet rooted to the ground by some bizarre suction as her mind completed the puzzle.

He knew about the passage. At his mention of the treasure, his eyes glowed with the light of obsession. He was educated, from York, and slept in an alcove near the buttery, whence the wine was stolen. He was jovial and unassuming, and like a spider spinning its geometrically precise web, he had orchestrated it all.

"Does Juliana know of your treachery?"

He quirked an eyebrow and walked along the inner edge of the circle. "I talk not of treachery, but treasure."

"And I'm talking about murder."

He halted and flashed a sardonic smile. "So you've

figured it out, have you?"

Unable to speak, she nodded.

He folded his arms. "Juliana knows nothing about it, nor will she. Once I have the treasure, we can be married. Heaven knows, I've searched long enough for it. Those fairy lights along the cliff Giles sings about…they were my torches on numerous trips down to the cave."

"Ranulf, listen to me. You found nothing because there *was* nothing. Simon was talking about Lillian, Lady Seacrest. *She* was his treasure."

"You're lying."

"Why would I?"

His hands dropped to his sides. "Because you love that great oaf of a baron and want to protect his secret. Many times, I listened outside the solar, waiting for him to confide in you. He must've done so elsewhere."

Argh! He was the most pigheaded person she'd ever met. But she needed answers, and he was the only one who could give them. "Why did you send me to the sea cave that last night?"

He grinned. "I knew you'd come if you thought Lady Seacrest was in danger. I intended to force information from you, but wanted help. So I divulged my plan to the archdeacon, offering him a share of the riches in exchange for his aid and Juliana's hand in marriage. He was perfectly agreeable until I mentioned torture."

She almost gagged. He was some actor. Never would she have guessed him capable of such depravity.

"The poor fellow said he had no taste for torture, and I could tell from his shifty eyes, he wanted out of our arrangement. Well, I couldn't let him blow the trumpet on me, so I pushed him over the cliff. Then I waited half a lifetime in the sea cave, but you didn't show. So I went to the wool barn, where I found Juliana sound asleep." His face softened. "When I woke her, she pledged her love for me."

"Why did you send her to the barn in the first place?"

"I had to get her out of your chamber to leave you the message. Her sister, of course, had already left the hall with Lady Seacrest." He fell silent and stared at her for several seconds. Then he heaved a long sigh. "Why don't you tell me what you know and be done with it?"

"I already have, Ranulf. Can I speak plainer? All I want is to go home; *that* was the treasure to which I referred."

He looked around him. "These stones are not your home."

"No, but they'll take me thither."

He crossed his arms again. "I've no idea what you mean, but I'm afraid you cannot go. Even if you don't know where the treasure is, I can use you to bargain with his lordship. Any threat to that pretty neck of yours should loosen his tongue."

A flutter sounded among the trees. Then a barn owl glided into view and settled on the stone nearest Ardyth.

A strange blend of peace and awe came over her as she looked up at it. *Are you the owl from Seacrest?*

But that was crazy. Impossible. Still, she felt drawn to the bird, compelled to meet its gaze.

Words flowed into her mind. *Walk through the gateway. Go now!*

****

'Twas the longest ride of Hugh's life. All the way north, his mind filled with imaginary scenes of violence and loss. Nonetheless, he refused to believe Ardyth was gone, to either her heavenly reward or a different time. Neither option was bearable.

He rode hard, stopping only to relieve himself and to change horses in Durham. At last, Ravenwood came into view. Hope and fear battled for his heart as he covered the remaining ground.

As expected for this time of the evening, the drawbridge was up. Atop the gatehouse, on the other side of the moat, a sentry peered down at him through the gap between two merlons.

He curbed his horse, raised a hand, and called to the guard. "Hail fellow!"

"Who goes there?"

"Lord Ravenwood's brother, Lord Seacrest. I seek not entrance but information. Where is Woden's Circle?"

The sentry stepped aside, and a familiar form took his place. "Hugh?"

"William!"

Another head appeared over William's shoulder. "Hugh! What the devil—"

"Robert!" Hugh sighed as hope took a stronghold. The sight of his brothers bestowed new life on his sleep-deprived mind and body. "Lady Ardyth is in trouble, and I believe she's gone to Woden's Circle. Where is it?"

Robert and William regarded one another. Then the former called down to him. "Wait there. We'll show you."

"Bring your swords. And fetch one for me while

you're at it!"

His brothers backed away from the parapet. Soon after, the portcullis groaned to life, and the drawbridge lowered. He dismounted as William and Robert urged their destriers, Thunder and Belfry, across the bridge.

William threw him a belt with scabbard and sword attached. "You found us atop the gatehouse because one of my men reported a man and woman riding east."

Hugh whipped the belt around his waist. "When?"

"Moments before you arrived."

"If the circle is to the east, the riders must've been Ranulf and Ardyth." With quick fingers, he fastened the belt.

Robert knitted his brow. "Ranulf the goliard? What threat does he pose?"

"He has slain Archdeacon Dominy."

"No great loss there."

"No indeed," William agreed.

"He also plotted against me, and now he's with Ardyth. I fear for her life." Hugh leapt onto his mount.

William's black eyes narrowed. "Then come, Brothers. To Woden's Circle!"

Of one mind, they galloped toward their goal. Just before the circle, they reined in their horses beside the other two and jumped to the ground.

Hugh's heart pounded as he gripped the hilt of his sheathed sword. With William to his right and Robert to his left, he entered the site.

His focus shot to the stone doorway. Ardyth was backing through it. Their gazes locked. Her eyes widened, and she disappeared.

His gut wrenched. *She's gone!* Back to her own time, as predicted. Every word she'd spoken was true, and he'd forsaken her.

Ranulf rushed to the gateway. "What?!"

"Halt where you stand!" William commanded.

The goliard froze. Slowly, he turned to face them.

A collective hiss sliced the air as the brothers drew their swords. As one, they pointed their blades toward the villain.

Hugh grimaced. "The game is up, Ranulf."

The cornered man attempted a smile. "Game?"

"Abduction. Assault. Murder. And a vain attempt to steal a nonexistent treasure."

"Treasure?" said Robert. "Don't tell me he thought there *was* one."

"'Tis real!" Ranulf spat.

William guffawed. "In your dreams, perhaps. But I'll tell you what *is* real: the walls of my prison tower."

Ranulf glowered at Hugh. "You have no proof of any wrongdoing."

A muscle worked in Hugh's jaw. "I have enough, and I'll see you hang." He glanced at William, then Robert. "Watch him, Brothers."

He strode to the gateway and circled it. Ardyth had vanished, without a single sign she'd ever been there.

He swallowed the lump in his throat and advanced toward Ranulf from the side. "Toss your dagger aside."

Ranulf fingered his weapon, then pulled it from its scabbard. "If death be my fate, it shall also be yours!" He spun toward Hugh and lunged.

Hugh dodged the attack and thrust his sword into Ranulf's stomach, running him through. He released the hilt, and the goliard fell forward, landing in a heap on the ground with the sword's tip protruding from his back.

He coughed up blood. "If only you'd...told me..." He winced. "...where...'twas hidden."

Hugh shook his head. "For the last time, there was no treasure. At least, none you'd understand."

A gurgle erupted from deep in Ranulf's throat. Then he stilled.

Hugh regarded his brothers, who sheathed their swords one after the other. "Thank you for your assistance."

William gave him a nod. "If only we'd been able to assist with Lady Ardyth. 'Twas she who disappeared, I take it."

Hugh sighed. "Aye."

Robert looked from his older brother to his oldest. "Then you both saw her too. I didn't just imagine it."

"May an old woman intrude?" Approaching his brothers from behind, an aged lady in gray with a flowing veil and a leather purse clutched in her hands entered the circle.

They both turned to her and spoke simultaneously. "Meg."

William shared a wry grin with Robert, then cleared his throat. "Lady Margaret, may I present my brother, Lord Seacrest?" He regarded Hugh. "Lord Seacrest, this is Lady Ravenwood's great-grandaunt, Lady Margaret."

"Please, call me Meg." Advancing toward him, she walked between his brothers and stopped an arm's length away. "I've waited ages for this meeting, Hugh."

He blinked at the familiarity. "I confess, I've wanted to meet you, as well."

She handed him the purse. "I found this tied to the lady's saddle. Open it."

"Very well." He did as she asked and eyed its contents.

The essentials for cleaning teeth. Two finely carved, double-sided combs. And...

His heart twisted. *The owl-feather quill. I hurt her deeply and still, she wanted to remember me.*

No! He couldn't be just a memory. He needed to be present, beside her, every day. Holding her close and feeling her arms around him. Sharing her thoughts, her highs and lows...her life! Any other future was intolerable.

His throat ached, and he forced himself to swallow. "Pray, tell me...what do you know of Lady Ardyth?"

Her violet eyes shone with sympathy. "My dear boy, I know more than you can possibly imagine. Come. Let's seek the comfort of the keep. We have much to discuss." She aimed significant looks at William and then Robert. "In private."

Hugh followed her to the circle's edge, where she paused and glanced up at a barn owl atop one of the stones. For the first time, he noticed the creature, and a number of ravens as well.

Meg smiled at the owl. "Good work," she praised. Then she turned her gaze to the west and carried on.

Chapter Eighteen

Oh my God! Ardyth couldn't believe her eyes. It was Hugh, standing between Robert and another man who had to be Lord Ravenwood.

As she stepped backward, heat swept through her body, and the vibration took hold. The next instant, the brothers and Ranulf disappeared.

The vibration ceased. Stunned and alone, she circled the gateway.

Why had Hugh been there? Had he come to capture a criminal? He might still see her as one. However much she wanted his trust, she realized her story sounded absurd.

An important message the wind just happened to blow away. Time travel. A female attending a "western" university, for he surely hadn't envisioned her as a student at the University of Constantinople. Magical stairs. A magic circle. What else should she have added? Puff the Magic Dragon?

Jeez! He must've thought I was batshit crazy!

Or…

Was there a chance he'd been there because he believed her? Had he come to make amends?

She sank to her knees and bowed her head. *I'll never know. I'll never see him again.*

Tears pricked her eyes, and this time she let them flow. She sobbed, surrounded by a stone ring which had carried her "home." Yet the only home she craved was Seacrest, and it was lost to her. So was its master.

Hugh! I'll always love you!

When the tears dried up and her abdominal muscles ached from her crying, she stood and brushed the dirt from her tunic. She still had her parents. And friends. And a budding career…no matter how hollow it seemed at this moment.

But she wouldn't have love. At least, not with Hugh.

Not with anyone! If she couldn't have Hugh, she didn't want another man. Ever. There was no one in all the world like him. Not in this time or any other.

Her mind made up, she strode out of the circle and down to the road. She raised her gaze to the ruin that was Ravenwood. Apart from intermittent wounds, most of the curtain wall was intact. The gatehouse had fared worse, ravaged by eight hundred and eighty-four years which she'd traversed in two seconds.

How long since she'd ridden past? Forty-five minutes? An hour?

The horse. Her purse! She'd meant to go back for it, until Ranulf showed his true self. After that, escape was foremost in her mind.

She blew out a long, defeated breath. Jocelyn's combs and Hugh's gift were gone forever.

A motor hummed to her left, and she started. A car! An Austin Mini, from the look of it. It sounded so foreign after what seemed a lifetime in the medieval world.

She stepped into the road and waved her hands. The car stopped, and she hastened to the driver's side window.

The sandy-haired woman behind the wheel appeared to be in her forties. "Hello, love. You look absolutely gutted. Can I help?"

She was blunt, friendly, and a godsend, for she was headed in the direction of Prestby and happy to share the short drive with a "medieval reenactor" who'd clearly been weeping. She also provided valuable information: the date was August 17, 1986, a little less than a month since Ardyth had climbed Woden's Stair.

When they entered the town of Prestby, Ardyth reflected on the advancements of transportation. How simple to jump in a car and zip to your destination in minutes, compared to riding on horseback for hours. There was much to be said for modern convenience.

But she'd give it all up for one more day with Hugh.

Nightshade Manor was awash with the subdued light of a summer's evening. The Samaritan driver dropped her off at the gates, then sped away.

Her pulse quickened as she followed the driveway up to the house. The windows of the long gallery glowed with electric light. What decadence to conjure light with the flip of a switch.

Henri must still be here. Did he freak out when she disappeared from Woden's Stair? Did he notify her parents? What should she tell him?

"Guess what? I met your ancestor, and we had one hell of a time together!"

Good lord. There was no simple way to start that conversation.

Within its flattened-arch Tudor frame, the oaken door waited for her next move. She took a deep breath and knocked.

No answer.

She knocked again, harder this time.

There was movement inside. Footfalls drew near, and the door swung open.

Henri filled the doorway. His intense gaze stole her breath. Had it not been for his short hair and modern clothes, he could *be* Hugh.

"Ardyth! You are well!" The voice was the same, too. How strange to hear him speak Modern English. "Come in."

He ushered her into the entrance hall and closed the door. Frowning, he studied her face. "Have you been crying?"

Crying? I just released the Niagara Falls of tears. "Yes."

His gray eyes overflowed with compassion. "I have something for you which might help." He disappeared into the sitting room and returned with…

A quill pen. *The* quill pen!

She gasped. "What?"

He handed it to her. "It is yours, is it not?"

"Yes, but how did you…Henri?"

His smile was tender, and his eyes sparkled with an inner light. "Actually, I am Hugh."

****

She gaped at him. He held his breath, waiting for her to speak.

After an endless moment, she blinked. "You've got some serious explaining to do."

Solemnly, he nodded. "But first, I must apologize." He took her free hand and clasped it with both of his. "I never should have doubted you, and I never will again. Can you forgive me?"

She hesitated, and tears welled in her eyes. "Of course, I can." She blinked rapidly and sniffed. "I didn't think I had any tears left. Hold on, let me put this down." She placed the quill on a table, wiped her eyes, and hurried back to him.

He encircled her waist with his hands. "Ardyth…I have waited so long to tell you…" He swallowed hard and stared into her infinite brown eyes. His future—all he ever hoped to be—glistened within them. "I love you."

Her lips quivered. Then she smiled. "And I love you."

He pulled her into his embrace and kissed her with all the passion and pain his heart had borne in the months since they'd separated, for several months had passed in *his* experience. Every fear, every risk was worth this blessed moment. Her touch, her kiss, her smile: they were everything.

He breathed in her scent and drew back, keeping her safely locked in his arms. He'd never let her go again. "Ranulf was behind it all."

"Yes, I know." Her hands rested on his chest. "How did you?"

"Giles."

"Really?" She knitted her brow. "I suppose you and your brothers imprisoned Ranulf."

He shook his head. "He attacked me at Woden's Circle, and I defended myself. He is dead."

"Thank God you're okay." She sighed. "Poor Juliana."

"She will recover…at home in York with Isobel."

"Isobel's in York?"

"My mother sent her away the day you left. She

knew, as I did, only one woman belonged at my side."

She gave him a shy grin. "Me?"

He nodded, and caressed her silken cheek. "Would you consider returning to Seacrest with me…for good?"

Her eyes widened. "Are you saying what I think you're saying?"

"I believe I am. Dearest, sweetest Ardyth, will you marry me?"

"Yes!" She flung her arms around his neck and kissed him hard on the mouth.

His ardor rose, but he pulled back slightly. "What about your career? I know it means a great deal to you."

"You mean more, and I'll be *living* medieval history! I can still write your family's saga, but now it'll be *my* family and my story, too." She beamed up at him, and his heart swelled. "Hugh, I'm so happy."

He cleared his throat. "There are two here who would share our happiness." He raised his voice. "You may come in now."

Mr. and Mrs. Nightshade emerged from the sitting room. While Ardyth had the gentleman's blond hair and brown eyes, her facial features were her mother's. But the lady's hair was black as a winter's night.

Ardyth gasped. "Mom? Dad?" Her joy overflowed in laughter as she broke away from Hugh and hugged each of her parents in turn. "What are you doing here? Did he tell you I disappeared?"

Mrs. Nightshade smiled at her daughter. "He did, but we knew it would happen. Do you remember when you were a little girl and you tried to climb the stairs up at the runestone?"

"How could I forget? You snatched me up so fast, I knew it scared you. We moved away soon after. Was that why?"

Mr. Nightshade nodded. "We couldn't risk losing you. Not then, at any rate."

His wife brushed a strand of hair from Ardyth's forehead. "You're everything to us, and we wanted to keep you in this time for as long as possible. But I knew from the moment you were born, you'd live the bulk of your life in the twelfth century."

Ardyth's jaw dropped. "How? One of your prophetic dreams?"

"Yes, when the doctor put me under for the C-section."

Her husband put an arm around her. "After she told me about the dream, we did a little research and found documentation to confirm it."

Ardyth raised her eyebrows. "What kind?"

"The family history you wrote…and will continue writing once you return…survived. Also, your marriage to Hugh, Lord Seacrest, was recorded in 1102, and soon afterward, the births of your children."

"Griff!" His wife looked sharply at him. "Shh!"

"Children?" Ardyth looked to Hugh, then back at her father. "How many?"

"I'm not saying another word! Your mom's right. It isn't good to know too much about your own future. I didn't tell Hugh, either, and didn't let him see any of the records or documents. Anyway, knowing your place in history was set, we did our best to prepare you. We spoke Anglo-Norman and Anglo-Saxon with you as often as possible, and I fostered your interest in the medieval period."

"You sure did! By the way, I met your ancestors, Wulfstan and Jocelyn. They were amazing!"

His eyes lit up. "I wish I'd been there with you."

"You would've loved it. But wait a minute." She turned to Hugh. "You still haven't told me how you came to be here in this time, or why you pretended to be Henri, or—"

"Listen and I will tell you. After you vanished at Woden's Circle, I met Meg of Ravenwood, and I asked her if it was possible to follow you into the future and bring you back. She said it was crucial for me to do so. She also explained that the energy surrounding the circle and Woden's Stair had intelligence, that it knew exactly when...namely, to what date and time...a person was meant to travel, and I must trust it to guide me to you. She and my brothers went with me to the circle the next evening and saw me off. Apparently, the night before, she met your mother in a dream and alerted her to my imminent arrival in this time."

Ardyth turned to her mother. "*You* met the infamous Meg? I was there, and I still haven't met her!"

Mrs. Nightshade grinned. "Don't worry. I'm sure you will soon. She told me the Lord Seacrest we'd discovered in our research would travel via Woden's Circle to the modern day, and we must be there to meet him. She gave me the precise date and time of his arrival: the tenth of May, just after Vespers." She looked to her husband.

Mr. Nightshade nodded. "Around seven p.m. at that time of year. She told your mom to teach Hugh the language of this time and to keep his true identity a secret from you, until you returned from the twelfth century yourself. So we hopped on a plane, met him at the circle, and brought him here to the manor, where we spent the next month teaching him Modern English and coming up with his cover story."

Ardyth gasped. "Your extended trip to Europe! You were here all the time."

"Yup. We left him here to continue his English studies while we returned to the States in time to set the hook."

"With a fictitious summer job you knew I couldn't refuse."

"We had to make it irresistible. Otherwise, you'd have accepted that German fellowship, and we wouldn't be standing here today."

Ardyth bit her lip and looked from one parent to the other. "But where do we go from here? Hugh and I will return to the twelfth century, but what about you guys? I can't stand the thought of never seeing you again."

Her mother's eyes glittered with unshed tears. "My beautiful girl…we want you to be happy, and you *will* be with Hugh in the twelfth century. Rest assured, we'll see each other again."

"When? Did you have another dream? Will you guys travel back in time, too? Dad would *love* that!"

"Yes. He would." Mrs. Nightshade swapped soulful looks with her husband. Then she gave their daughter a tender smile. "Just trust me. You'll see us sooner than you think."

Chapter Nineteen

For two days, Ardyth savored everything the modern world had to offer. Quality time with her parents. Potatoes, chocolate, ice cream, tea, coffee, and pop. Electric lights, the cinema, TV, and radio. A toothbrush, toothpaste, hot showers, a flushing toilet, and toilet paper. A firm yet cushiony mattress, of which she and Hugh made good use...quietly, since her parents slept just down the hall.

When the big day arrived, she smoothed the skirt of her newly washed medieval gown, cast a bittersweet glance at the en suite bathroom they'd shared, and paraphrased Shakespeare. "Good night, sweet loo, and flights of angels sing thee to thy rest."

Looking dashing in his medieval clothes, Hugh cocked an eyebrow. "What?"

"I'm just bidding a fond farewell to the toilet. Of course, it'll live on long after we're gone."

"I do admit, the first time I heard a flush, it startled me." He grinned. "But only you would speak of a toilet as if it were alive."

"I can do no less, for it has served me well."

He chuckled, then gave her a sympathetic look. "I understand your sorrow at parting with it. No garderobe was ever so fine." With sudden intensity, he embraced her. "When we return to Seacrest, I will shower you with luxuries."

Her heart was full as she ran her fingers through his silky hair. "I've found all the luxury I could ever need in your arms."

Said arms tightened around her, and he kissed her passionately. Then he lifted his head and guided her toward the bedroom door. "Come. The moment has arrived."

Minutes later, they stood with her parents beside Woden's Stair. A cool morning breeze caressed the glade and all within it.

Her heart twisted. "I love you, Mom. I love you, Dad." She hugged them tightly.

Her mother blinked back tears. "We love you too. I put a photo of your dad and me in Hugh's purse." She gestured to the leather pouch attached to his belt, which also contained the owl-feather quill. "Something to remember us by, until we meet again."

Her father took a deep breath and released it. "Be well, sweetheart." He regarded Hugh. "Take care of her, Son."

Hugh gave him a nod. "I will. Thank you both for everything." He gave Ardyth a look of adoration that stirred her soul. "And I do mean everything."

He offered her his hand, and she took it. Together, they climbed the stone stairs and paused on the landing for a final glimpse of her parents.

"Good-bye," she said.

Arms locked around each other, her parents spoke as one. "Good-bye."

Hugh turned to her. "Fear not. You're safe with me."

She smiled, recalling their "date" in the valley when she'd said those same words to him. She repeated his response now. "Am I?"

His gaze held hers. "Always."

Hand in hand, they stepped forward. Tingling heat spread through her body, and the force beyond comprehension whisked them to a dawn eight centuries before.

"I told you they were coming!" It was Freya's voice, sounding behind them at ground level.

Ardyth released Hugh's hand and turned. Freya, Jocelyn, and Wulfstan stood waiting at the base of the stairs. "Good morrow! Or is it evening?"

Jocelyn beamed up at them. "No, 'tis morning."

Ardyth hurried down the steps and hugged all three of her startled relatives. When Hugh's feet touched ground, she made the introductions and smiled. "'Tis wonderful to see you all again. Is the year still eleven hundred and two?"

Wulfstan grinned. "Aye, and welcome. Ever since Meg wrote to us of your journey…both your journeys…we've awaited your return. Then a short while ago, at daybreak, Freya informed us your arrival was nigh."

Hugh shook his head. "Extraordinary." He turned to Ardyth. "But after all we've experienced, I suppose anything is possible."

Jocelyn shared a meaningful glance with her husband. "I learned that lesson well enough when I first came hither. Speaking of the impossible made real, Ravenwood has a son!"

Hugh's eyes widened. "My brother is a father. What glad tidings! And Lady Ravenwood?"

"She is well and expecting our visit. Sir Robert and Lady Constance are there already, and they're all most anxious to see you, Ardyth. Meg revealed your true origins to them, so prepare yourself for a barrage of questions when next you meet. I wrote to Lady Ravenwood that we'd wait until you both arrived before visiting."

"And here you are!" Freya bounced up and down, then turned a shy grin on Hugh. "You must go with us and meet your nephew."

He gave her a winning smile. "Indeed, I must."

Wulfstan gently tugged his sister's blonde braid. "As usual, you're correct." He linked hands with Jocelyn. "Come, everyone. To the keep."

With a flourish, Freya pointed southward. "And to Ravenwood!"

By day's end, the party arrived at Ravenwood Keep. Lord and Lady Ravenwood, Sir Robert, and Lady Constance all came out to the courtyard to greet them. During the introductions, Ardyth couldn't help staring at Lady Ravenwood, or Emma, as William and Wulfstan called her. With her black hair and violet eyes, she looked so like her own mother.

Genetics at work again, she thought. Still, there was something about her...

She shrugged it off. Until she noticed Hugh's gaze riveted on Emma, too.

William raised an eyebrow. "Hugh, why do you stare at my wife?"

Hugh blinked. "Forgive me. 'Tis only that..." He turned to Ardyth. "Her resemblance to your mother is astonishing."

Ardyth nodded. "I was just thinking the same thing. Do you have the picture of my parents?"

"I do." He reached into his leather pouch, withdrew

the photo, and handed it to Ardyth. It was one of her favorites, taken just after her parents were married.

Robert popped behind them and looked over their shoulders. "I say! 'Tis incredible...both the likeness and the quality of the painting."

Constance pushed him out of the way to take a peek herself. "Wondrous!"

Ardyth smiled. "'Tisn't a painting but an actual moment frozen in time and recorded on a substance a little like parchment."

William frowned. "Let us see." He took the photo from Hugh. Jocelyn, Wulfstan, and Freya crowded around the couple for a glimpse.

Emma gasped. "It cannot be!"

Her husband turned to her. "What is it?"

"I've seen this woman many times in my visions. She's my mother!"

Ardyth knitted her brow. "But my lady, she's *my* mother."

Robert made a face. "She cannot be mother to you both."

"Meg will know the answer!" Freya laid a hand on Emma's arm. "Where is she?"

Emma thought for a moment. "When last I saw her, she was in the solar."

Freya grabbed Emma's hand. "Let's see if she's still there."

Finally! The elusive Meg. Ardyth glanced at Hugh. He gave her a puzzled look, then shrugged and took her hand. Together, they followed the others into the keep and to the lord's solar.

A woman in a long veil stood within. Her back turned, she stared up at a striking tapestry of lords and ladies dancing around a bonfire.

Ardyth squeezed Hugh's hand, then released it. On impulse, she inched in front of the others.

Emma did the same. "Meg?"

The old woman turned. Her eyes glistened with emotion barely contained. "Emma. Ardyth. Together at last."

Her voice. Her eyes. The tilt of her head. All were familiar to Ardyth, for she'd known them all her life.

Oh my God. "Mom?"

Meg nodded. "Hi, honey." She spoke in perfect Modern English.

"What the..." Ardyth switched back to Anglo-Norman so the others would understand. "How is this possible?"

"You're Meg Nightshade?" Hugh moved to stand beside Ardyth. "I noticed similarities, but I never dreamed..."

Meg smiled. "Why would you?" Her violet gaze shifted to Emma. "And now it can be told. Dearest Emma, I'm your mother."

Emma gaped at her in silence.

"You?" William rushed to Emma's side and put an arm around her. "Meg, why did you not say so before? All this time..."

"I wanted to," said Meg. "You've no idea how much."

The full implications hit Ardyth. "I have a sister!"

Emma turned and met her gaze. They shared tentative smiles, then regarded their mother again.

Meg clasped her hands in front of her. "I had to keep my secret until both my daughters were here." She looked at Ardyth. "Until you were safely back in this time for good."

Emma leaned into William's embrace. "I have so many questions."

Ardyth nodded. "So do I. The dream…when you supposedly met Meg…I mean you…"

Meg grinned. "I paid my younger self a visit."

Constance gasped, looked to Robert, then returned her gaze to Meg. "You once told us the soul could be in many places at once."

"Aye," said Robert. "We learned that firsthand. It seems you did too, Meg."

Meg gave him a droll look. "You've no idea."

"Perhaps not, but I want to."

"As do I," Wulfstan remarked.

Ardyth smiled to herself. *Join the club!*

Meg's violet eyes twinkled with love, light, and a hint of mischief. "Then gather round, my dears, and I'll tell you a story…"

A word about the author...

Judith Sterling is an award-winning author whose love of history and passion for the paranormal infuse everything she writes. Whether penning medieval romance (*The Novels of Ravenwood*) or young adult paranormal fantasy (the *Guardians of Erin* series), her favorite themes include true love, destiny, time travel, healing, redemption, and finding the hidden magic which exists all around us. She loves to share that magic with readers and whisk them far away from their troubles, particularly to locations in the British Isles.

Her nonfiction books, written under Judith Marshall, have been translated into multiple languages. She has an MA in linguistics and a BA in history, with a minor in British Studies. Born in that sauna called Florida, she craved cooler climes, and once the travel bug bit, she lived in England, Scotland, Sweden, Wisconsin, Virginia, and on the island of Nantucket. She currently lives in Salem, Massachusetts with her husband and their identical twin sons.

http://judithmarshallauthor.com

Thank you for purchasing
this publication of The Wild Rose Press, Inc.

For questions or more information
contact us at
info@thewildrosepress.com.

The Wild Rose Press, Inc.
www.thewildrosepress.com

To visit with authors of
The Wild Rose Press, Inc.
join our yahoo loop at
http://groups.yahoo.com/group/thewildrosepress/